———✦———

H E HAD ALWAYS looked at her with kindness and compassion, but now there was something of possessiveness in his face that she was not sure she liked.

"Your kingdom," said Chala, trying to move his attention away from herself and back where it belonged. "It waits for you. Or do you not care about that anymore?"

Richon flushed. "I care about it. I care about nothing else."

Not entirely the truth, but perhaps as much as he was willing to say aloud. That was the way it was with humans.

Also by Mette Ivie Harrison

The Princess and the Hound
The Princess and the Snowbird

Mira, Mirror
The Monster in Me

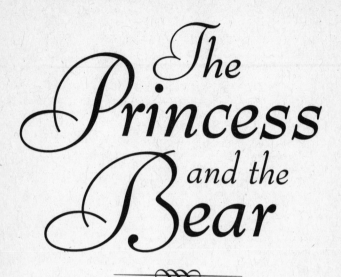

The
Princess
and the
Bear

Mette
Ivie
Harrison

HARPER TEEN
An Imprint of HarperCollinsPublishers

HarperTeen is an imprint of HarperCollins Publishers.

The Princess and the Bear
For information address HarperCollins Children's Books,
a division of HarperCollins Publishers,
10 East 53rd Street, New York, NY 10022.
www.harperteen.com

Library of Congress Cataloging-in-Publication Data
Harrison, Mette Ivie, 1970–
 The princess and the bear / Mette Ivie Harrison. — 1st ed.
     p.   cm. [Sequel to: The princess and the hound.]
 Summary: A hound who was once a princess and a bear who was
once a king travel back in time to save a kingdom and find their human
selves.
 ISBN 978-0-06-155316-5
 [1. Fairy tales.   2. Princesses—Fiction.   3. Kings, queens, rulers,
etc.—Fiction.   4. Human-animal communication—Fiction.   5. Time
travel—Fiction.   6. Magic—Fiction.]   I. Title.
PZ8.H248 Prh   2009   2008031144
[Fic]—dc22   CIP
                                                   AC

10 11 12 13 14 LP/RRDH 10 9 8 7 6 5 4 3 2 1
❖
First paperback edition, 2010

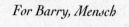

For Barry, Mensch

PROLOGUE

The Tale of the Cat That Became a Man

L ONG AGO, THERE lived a wild cat that was the sleekest, fastest, and bravest of its kind. It had been triumphant in battles against the most fearsome beasts of the forest: bear and elk and charging moose. But it was said to have an uncanny intelligence and a look to the eyes that was almost human. Those who had seen it claimed that the wild cat would even leap straight through a bonfire or dive into a river's raging water to get at its prey.

Legends grew up around the wild cat, which was known by the striping around its nose, and humans sought to prove their prowess against it. But no matter how often it was hunted, the wild cat was never caught. Arrows were not fast enough and swords slid past it. Those who rode against it did not return—or returned very different men from when they had gone out.

One day, a young student of magic decided to go into

the forest to see if even half of the stories he had heard about the wild cat were true. He found its trail and followed it. Then, with his own eyes, he saw the wild cat kill two deer in one leaping attack and defend itself against a pack of hounds that came against it in an attempt to take its prey. Two of the hounds were dead in the few moments it took for the rest of them to decide to retreat, and many more were injured in the battle.

The young man watched the cat carry off the carcasses, one after the other, to its lair. And then, late that evening, he heard a soft, warbling sound coming from the place where the wild cat had gone.

The student followed the sound until he had reached a small cave hidden behind a waterfall. He climbed to the entrance, then poked his head inside to see the wild cat playing a flute made out of bone. The bone had been hollowed out and the young man of magic could see strewn on the floor of the cave other similar flutes, perhaps of different tones, and even one lyre.

The student could hardly believe his eyes. A cat that could play an instrument stolen from a human was one thing. But a cat that could make the instrument? That was extraordinary indeed!

Now the student spread forth his hands and let the heat of his magic flow out. The wild cat made one strangled yelp before the magic overcame it, and then it began to change.

Slowly—one paw at a time, then a nose and an ear and a haunch—the wild cat was transformed into a tall, graceful man with tawny hair and faintly striped skin around the nose.

The young man of magic expected the new cat man to be pleased. He offered his own jacket and a few coins to help the cat man on his way.

"There is a town some miles south, past the edge of the forest," the young man of magic explained in the language of the wild cats. "I am sure you will find all you need for comfort there."

He nodded to the cat man and told himself that soon the wild cat would learn to speak as humans did. Then the student went on his way, proud of his success with such great and powerful magic.

But the cat man was not happy. He could not remain in the forest, for a man's hands were too soft for the kill and a man's teeth could not tear and rend flesh. He could not speak the language of the wild cats, for he no longer had the right shape to his tongue, teeth, and mouth. He tried to make the same sounds, but they came out tuneless and wrong.

He had no choice but to do as the student had bid him and leave the forest where he had felt himself the most magnificent of all animals. The journey through the forest was painful and slow, for the student had left him no boots, and his tender man's feet were badly blistered in a few hours' time. His uncovered legs stung from too much sun and scrapes from the tree branches that seemed to grab at him.

At last the cat man arrived at an inn in the nearest town. Here, once he showed his coins, he was cared for, despite his lack of speech. He was given clothing and as much food and drink as he wished. Also a warm bed, soft blankets, and music far more beautiful than he had ever produced himself.

For a time he stopped longing for the forest and the life that had been his. He simply enjoyed each moment, for that is the way that a cat is, and every animal. Men might think of the future or the past, but for animals there is only this moment, and then the next one.

But it was not long before the few coins that the student of magic had given the cat man were gone. Evicted from the inn, he was thrown into the streets of the town and began to live as a beggar and a thief. He attacked passersby without compunction, combining a man's clever hands with a cat's vicious speed, and soon he was proud of having killed as many in the town as in the forest.

So it was that the student, returning to the town with his masters in his carriage, showed the proof of his talents, but not in the way he had expected.

The cat man leaped at the carriage with all aboard, growling and clawing and gnashing his teeth. The young man trembled, realizing he had transformed the wild cat into a man without respect for what he had been or understanding of what he would become.

He tried to pretend that he knew nothing of the creature, but the tawny hair and striped face gave the cat man's identity away. The masters were horrified at what the student had done and told him they would not teach him another day.

Angry, the young man turned on the fleeing cat man and caught his legs with magic. They changed back into their animal form, though he left the rest of the cat man as he was.

"What has become of you? How can you have done this with the great gift that I offered you?" he complained.

The cat man spat and bit and scratched, but could not answer in any language.

The student stared at the cat man and saw in him the cause of his failure.

He lifted his hands and gathered his power, intending to reverse his magic. But the student had another idea for revenge. He used his magic to make the cat man look wholly human once more. Then he bound the cat man with ropes and took him home to be his servant. For many years they lived together, until, one day, the man was found dead in his own chambers.

The ropes he had used to keep his servant tethered to him had been broken, and of the servant himself there was no sign. But the man had been old, and there was no reason to suspect that there was anything to fear in the poor servant.

If some saw the strange servant roaming the forests and beyond, they said nothing of it. Nor did they connect the change in the forest itself, or in the other animals that lived within it, to the servant who had once been a cat man.

CHAPTER ONE

The Hound

THE SMELL OF the forest hit her first. Pine and moss and sweat-touched fur.

It was right again.

And so was she.

Her paws were on the ground. She could stretch her back and scratch herself as needed and she had a tail again to keep her balance.

She felt how strong and wide her jaw was now, and she tested her teeth by chomping at a branch of the tree at her side. It snapped instantly, cleanly, just as prey would when she was ready to chase it.

She could hear the distant call of a bird and the splash of a fish in the water not far away.

She tried out her strong legs and discovered she could run as fast as ever, leap over fallen trees, then turn around in a flick of movement and be racing back the same way again.

That was when she nearly careened into the bear.

And remembered why he was here.

The bear who had been a man, whose story she had heard when she was a princess.

The bear Prince George had brought her to, the one who had challenged her, then watched her change from woman to hound.

Where was Prince George? And the princess?

The hound had not seen them leave. She had been too busy rediscovering herself.

Now the bear sniffed in her direction.

She sniffed back and approached him slowly, head down, to show that she would not attack. Her lips twitched and she caught a snarl in her throat. The bear made a wordless sound like a groan, then gestured with one large paw toward the rocky part of the forest.

He took a step in that direction, then stopped. Waiting, but without threat.

She thought briefly of the year she had spent as human, when she had never been allowed to choose anything for herself. The boots she had had to wear, pinching her feet, the gowns that were "suitable," the words she was expected to say, the curtsying and smiling.

But that was gone.

She was a hound again. And the bear was an animal, as she was.

She lumbered cautiously alongside him as they crossed twice over a cold stream and approached a cave.

The bear entered it.

She moved across the rocks and peered inside.

The bear settled at one end of the cave and stretched out on the floor near the back with his side to the rock wall. She could smell water in the air. It was dripping on the bear, but he did not complain.

She moved forward, then tucked herself in close to him, letting her legs curl up underneath her. She could feel the brush of his fur against hers.

She shivered, then moved closer to the bear, until she could feel the hurried breathing of his chest against her.

Gradually it slowed. And she slept.

The next morning, as the two drank by the stream, a herd of rabbits crossed their path.

The hound held back, allowing the bear the first kill. But his attack was so loud and wide that by the time he had the first rabbit in his mouth, all the others had scattered.

The hound spent long minutes chasing them, but they were gone, and so was any other hope of game that morning. The woods were silent, the animals warned by the great noise of the bear and the lingering scent of death.

Angry, she returned to the stream, expecting the bear to have eaten his kill.

Yet the bear held out the rabbit, freshly cleaned in the stream and an hour dead.

She took half of the rabbit meat, and left the other

half for him. He must have been offering half as recompense for ruining her chance to get her own.

But the bear would not eat his half of the rabbit. He pushed it toward her.

She pushed it back to him and whined.

He turned away from it.

She growled at him. How could he be so stubborn? She knew he must be as hungry as she.

But he would not take it.

So she turned her back on the meat.

They went back to the cave, her stomach only half full and his entirely empty.

What was wrong?

She could speak the language of the hounds, but he could not. His mouth could only produce the language of the bears, which neither understood.

CHAPTER TWO

The Bear

T HE HOUND'S PRESENCE bothered the bear in small, petty ways, though he knew it should not.

She slept noisily, and sometimes her legs moved in the night as if she were running. She ate constantly and moved so quickly that it made his head ache.

He wished that she would simply sit beside him at the stream. Or nuzzle next to him in the cave at night until they both fell asleep together.

He had not thought it possible to feel even lonelier than he had before Prince George had worked his magic to make the hound a hound again, and the princess a woman. But he did.

It was worse still when he and the hound were called for the wedding a few weeks later, and they saw the joy in the eyes of Princess Marit and Prince George. The way that each seemed to see only the other, the whispers they shared with each other, the gentle laughter and instinctively coordinated steps.

Why could the bear not have the love that the prince had?

He had never been one to settle for second best. Over the last two hundred years, more than one she-bear had signaled with a rooting call and a turn of her flank that she had need of a mate and he would be a fine choice.

Had he been tempted? Perhaps a little. Having a warm body next to his, if nothing else, would have kept the cold of the winter nights away. Still, he had known it would have been a second best for both of them. A she-bear would be disappointed that he could not even speak as a bear and he wanted more than a warm body.

But the hound was not just a warm body. She was life and exuberance, freedom and grace. She was as fine a companion as he could have imagined having in the forest.

And yet . . . he could not say he loved her. There was something missing between them, something that George and Marit had. Something that the bear had never known but had always longed for.

One night, as the hound slept and he could see the spill of moonlight against her black form, the bear thought of the women whom he had believed he loved, when he was a king, and a man, and very young.

Lady Finick.

She had had the most beautiful blond hair. Her mouth

had been wide and very red, and when she was not smiling, she was laughing. And touching him. Leaning over him with her ample breasts, letting him smell the flowers in her hair, letting him feel her body against his.

Lady Trinner. She had been so petite that on first sight she had seemed a child. Then he had seen her bright eyes and the teasing flounce of her long black hair and gowns designed to make her tiny waist seem tinier still. She had been easy to dance with. One could hardly make a mistake as her partner.

Richon had been unable to choose between them. And why should he? He was king, was he not? Compromises and sacrifices were for others to make, not for him.

Then, one day, the royal steward had come to him with letters to prove Lady Finick was in a conspiracy with another man to steal from the royal treasury. When he confronted her, she did not try to deny it. She told him it was his own fault, for not marrying her soon enough, for not giving her access to the treasury himself.

Did she expect him to apologize for that? To offer to marry her then?

He listened to her screech at him, felt her spittle land on his cheeks, and told himself that he still had Lady Trinner.

But by then Lady Trinner had engaged herself to a duke from another kingdom, a man she had never met.

Fine, let her go, he thought. He did not care. He would

find another, better, brighter, prettier than she.

He said good-bye to Lady Trinner with cold formality, the lord chamberlain and royal steward at his side, looking on with approval at his restraint.

Hours later, he had given up his pride and leaped onto his fastest horse to chase after her. He caught her at the border of his country and begged her to stay with him.

She had looked him in the eyes and said, "But I could never love you. You are too shallow and selfish. You are a boy still, and I will not marry a boy."

Then she had climbed back into her carriage and gone on her way.

When he returned to his palace alone, Richon had tried frantically to prove to himself that she was wrong. He called for sad songs from minstrels and listened to the deep philosophers of the kingdom. He even gave offerings to a few beggars outside the palace, where before he had set the royal hounds on them to chase them out.

But he soon tired of such pursuits and sought an easier way to blot out Lady Trinner's memory: more ale and a series of days that ran into other days, indistinct and unending.

He began to believe he simply had no heart to give, and when the wild man had come with his army, he had thought that he would be given relief in death.

But the wild man had not taken his life. He had given him more life instead, an enchanted life as a bear that went on and on.

Now he understood poverty, hunger, desperation. He knew how selfish and thoughtlessly cruel he had been.

But love?

He had still not learned that.

Chapter Three

The Hound

SOMETIMES SHE HAD nightmares that she was human again.

She dreamed of the moment more than a year ago when Dr. Gharn had snarled at the princess, his face too close, his voice too loud.

She had growled at him, and then she had no longer been at the princess's side. She had had no idea where the princess was at all, but Dr. Gharn was in her face.

He smiled at her. She tried to leap at him but fell over. He laughed.

She could not get up. There was something wrong. Everything was wrong.

She made a strange yelping noise. And then there had been a hound next to her. A familiar hound, one she could smell and recognize. But the hound did not lick her. It stared at her and made its own sound of distress.

She had spent days in the princess's bedchamber,

alone, cowering under blankets whenever a maid entered with a tray of food that she could not bear to eat.

The hound prodded her to look at herself in a glass, see her human form. Together, using sign language, they had worked out the magic that Dr. Gharn had wreaked on them. She had accepted that it might never be undone, that she might remain in the body of a princess the rest of her life.

Prince George had saved her from that.

Now she was a hound once more—in body. But in mind?

If she still dreamed of being human, was there some part of her that had not returned to being a hound?

She dreamed of songs.

Stories.

Letters.

Even words carved into the stone of the palace.

And when she woke, there was silence with the bear.

The bear could not learn the sign language she had perfected with the princess. He was too old, perhaps. Or too used to living alone.

When winter came, she gave up trying to teach him. It frustrated them both, so they began to avoid each other. But they always returned to the cave at night.

The hound thought of some things that she missed about being human.

Music.

Lights.

The feel of thrice-carded wool against her nose.

And she was disgusted with herself. Those were soft things. She did not need them. She was a hound.

She did not need the bear, either. And she meant to prove it to herself.

The winter was long and killing cold. There was little to eat, and both the bear and hound grew thin.

The first night of spring, the hound went deep into the forest, to paths she remembered from her days with her own pack. She felt as if she had gone back in time to be that other hound. As if all her time with humans was washed from her.

It was a marvelous, free feeling.

She chased and chased, the heat of the run as glorious as the taste of fresh meat in her mouth.

When night struck, she crouched near a log and closed her eyes, ready to sleep. It was what she would have done before she met the princess, when she had been sent away from her pack and roamed the forest alone.

But she was not content.

She thought of the bear in the cave and how warm it was to sleep with him, how safe she felt with the sound of his breathing in her ears.

She dozed in fits and starts until the middle of the night, when she could sleep no more. She had to go back to the bear, to the cave. Home.

But it hurt to move. She ached all over from sore muscles.

It had been too long since she had spent so much time in a chase. And, she admitted to herself, she was getting older. She was no longer a young bitch hound, able to run all day without feeling ill effects.

In human years she was not old. She remembered eight full years of seasons.

But as a hound, she would at her age have had only one place remaining in a pack: to care for the pups of the lead mates. And even then, she would be given very little food indeed, for there were always more aging hounds than there was food to offer them.

To the bear, however, age and time were different than they were for any other creature, human or man. The bear had lived more than two hundred years, many times the lifetime of either a normal bear or a man. To him her age meant nothing.

Perhaps she did not need the bear, but that did not mean she did not miss him.

In the dark she struggled to make her way back through the forest. A few steps at a time, then resting as her sore paws found soft leaves. She was not lost, but she was glad when she found the familiar scent of the stream that ran near the cave. She was still some distance away, but now all she had to do was put her head down and follow the stream.

The cool water on her paws felt good, and even better when she let herself lie back on her haunches and cool the swollen muscles in her hind legs.

It was almost dawn when she caught sight of the cave. She stopped a long moment, then saw the bear at the mouth of the cave, standing upright and trembling.

She stepped back at the sight of him.

Was he angry?

She moved closer and he fell onto all fours and drew his face very close to hers.

She could feel his breath, and it might have been comforting but for the look of fierceness on his face.

She was sorry.

It was a strangely human thing to feel.

CHAPTER FOUR
The Bear

THE BEAR HAD only a moment to feel relief at the sight of the hound. Then he saw the danger.

Just beyond the hound were three bears, two smaller and one very large. A mother and cubs? If so, the cubs were nearly grown now, and they were just as dangerous as their mother.

The bears were tense, ready for action. At any moment they would attack the hound.

Yet she did not sense them.

He waved at her.

At last she turned and let out a deep growl in the base of her throat.

One of the bear cubs moved closer to threaten her.

It paid no attention to the hound's bear, seeing no reason to imagine an alliance between hound and bear.

They were natural enemies. The hound's bear had once been attacked by a pack of hounds at the end of winter, desperate for a meal and unaware of what it meant that a bear was not in hibernation.

Now it was spring and these bears had become the hunters, hungry for their first meal.

The mother bear was circling to the side.

Then the smaller of the two cubs slashed his claws at the hound's left hind leg.

She did not even cry out.

The hound's bear saw the blood streaming down her leg and into the dirt, and for one stunned moment he did not move. Then he flung himself forward, but she was ahead of him, closing in on the mother bear.

Was she trying to get herself killed?

Before he could intervene, the mother bear lunged at the hound and threw her across the stream. After the hound landed, she did not move.

The sight of her lifeless body, half in, half out of the stream, was more painful to the bear than he had imagined it could be.

"No!"

He wanted to shout, but all that came from his mouth was an inarticulate cry.

He charged again.

The other bears bellowed.

He struck the mother bear first, taking them both to the ground. The cubs leaped forward and sank their teeth into his skin, but he felt no pain.

His eyes were on the hound, who was still as death.

It had been a long time since he was so angry.

Not since he was a man and a king.

He threw the two cubs away from him so that they hit the ground hard and did not stand again for quite some time.

The mother bear rose and circled warily.

And then the hound moved. She did not stand, but she dragged herself from the stream.

She was alive!

The rush of violence faded.

After two deep breaths he turned back to the three bears, challenging them with his eyes to come after him.

They did not move.

So he put his back to the hound and retreated with her.

All three bears stood up on their hind legs as one last challenge, then fell and wandered away.

The hound dragged herself, refusing his help, back to the cave.

The bear brought leaves from the edge of the stream that he remembered from when he was a man and ill. The king's physician had made him eat a tea brewed from those leaves so that his fever would break. The hound would need them, too.

She turned her head away from the taste.

But the bear pushed them at her again, pressing them into her mouth.

She chewed the bitter leaves a few times, then spit them out.

The bear went back to the stream to get more.

At last she managed to swallow a few of them.

She slept, and when she woke the bear had brought her a possum, dripping with blood.

All those years he had not killed another creature, and now he did it without thinking. He told himself it was the way of the forest and watched as she bolted the carcass down.

Then he came closer and licked her wounds.

Chapter Five

The Hound

RECOVERING FROM THE wound with the bear so close to her, every moment of the day, was pleasant at first. She felt safe with him despite the pain. But when the pain turned to itching, the hound found herself more irritable. She nipped at him more than once and stopped thinking of him as the bear who had saved her. He was her tormenter, and she could do nothing but what he said she could.

At last, after several days of confinement, the bear let her go on her own past his line of sight. She had proven she was well enough to catch a fish in the stream while he was watching. Her hind leg was cleanly healed and she moved without any hesitation, even when leaping forward into the water.

The hound was not interested in looking back. She was free again, and it was as wonderful as it had been when the magic had released her.

She leaped and yelped and stood very still, holding her breath so that she could see the other creatures move around her. There was a butterfly dusting by in the faint breeze, as beautiful and delicate as life itself.

But by the end of an hour's play she was exhausted. She was not ready to return to the cave, so she wandered into the forest.

That was when she came across the strange trail. The first scent of it brought her up straight and unmoving, ready for attack. Then, slowly, as she realized there was no immediate danger, she divided the scent into the familiar and the unfamiliar.

The familiar was the trace of wild cat. She had not come across wild cats in this forest before, but farther north in the mountains that began at the end of the kingdom of Sarrey there were wild cats in plenty. They were mostly solitary creatures, not living in family groups or even clowders except when a mother had young children. This was a male wild cat, the hound was certain, but it was also something else.

The unfamiliar smell was far more troubling. It made her feel cold to the very bone. Her instincts screamed at her to leave, but she ignored them.

She looked around, determined to at least understand what was wrong here before she fled. This was her forest, and she would not be frightened from it.

There was a waterfall nearby, where a stream fell from one side of a crevice to the gully beneath. She found a rock wall to hide behind, and there she waited.

In time her nose lifted at the scent of the wild cat.

Then she looked and saw—it was a man.

At least, it wore a man's body.

Had it been enchanted, as she had been?

She held back and watched the cat man further.

He wore no shirt at all to cover his chest and shoulders. The hound herself was not cold in this weather, but she thought that a human must be. Yet she saw no sign of discomfort, no rubbing of hands or jumping in place to keep warm. Nor a fire, either.

Barefoot, the cat man's feet trailed some blood but were mostly hardened and callused as if he had gone a long while without shoes. He wore tattered trousers, but with his crouched stance, his furtive wanderings, his scent, he seemed even less human than she was.

The cat man drank at the stream a little farther down from the waterfall. He bent over and drank with his face fully in the water, then lifted it up and shook his head, exactly as a wild cat would do.

The hound could see then that there was a strange coloring around his face. He was very tanned, but in addition to this, she could see, were the faint marks of a golden striping around his nose.

The cat man lay flat on his stomach with his hands dangling in the water. It was fresh snowmelt, so the water was very cold, but the cat man kept his hands in for quite a while. Then, with an animal's swiftness and precision, he caught a fish and threw it into the air.

The hound would have expected that he would lift his head up and let the fish fall straight into his open mouth, as a wild cat would.

But it did not happen that way.

Instead the cat man grabbed the fish out of the air with one hand and smacked it against a rock near the stream. Not quite enough to kill it, but enough to render it paralyzed.

Helpless but still sensible, the hound thought.

The cat man then stooped over it and stared at it for a long while.

It wasn't until the hound was shivering that she realized he was doing more than just watching the motionless fish.

He was slowly draining it of whatever it was that made it alive. And smiling as he did so.

When he was finished, the color of the fish's scales had changed to a dead gray. But the damage extended beyond the fish. From as far away as the hound was, she could feel the difference in the forest itself. As if something had been ripped from not just the fish, but every living thing within a certain radius.

This was what she had smelled from the first, in addition to the smell of the wild cat.

It was all the hound could do not to gag at the feeling of terrible magic in the air. She thought she had seen the worst magic there was in Dr. Gharn's abominable use of it; she now knew that she was wrong.

The hound trembled, desperate to be away, to be out in full sunshine. She tried to keep very quiet. She was used to being a hunter and to stalking her prey. She should have been able to keep still.

But the cold that seeped into her bones was too much for her.

She made the smallest sound, like a moan, and the cat man's eyes turned toward her.

There was a wide smile on his face as his eyes seemed to catch her.

But the cat man was distracted by a deer that crossed between him and the hound. The deer froze as the hound had, and it was in that moment that the hound fled.

She heard the sound of a weight falling but no cry.

She ran and did not stop until she was at the cave once more, drenched in sweat and shaking so she could not stand.

The bear came close and touched her hind leg, in search of a reopened cut or a fever, but she ignored him.

Where had the cat man come from? She had never sensed anything like that cold death before, so the cat man had to be recently come to this part of the world. Where had it been before? What had it done?

She imagined the same cold death spread everywhere. She could not stop her mind from seeing a barren land stretching out before her. Was that why the cat man had come here? Had it destroyed all it could where it had been and now would do the same here?

Did it even know what it did?

She thought again of the cat man's face, the pleasure it showed in the fish's death.

It knew.

She looked up at the bear at last.

He made a motion with his paws, as if to offer to get a kill for her.

She shook her head and began to scratch in the dirt, making an elaborate map of the forest, beginning with the stream beside the cave and marking other places in the forest she and the bear both knew well. The place of the transformation, near the castle, the hills at the north, the streams that emptied into a river at the south.

Never before had she been so frustrated by the need for human words.

She tried to draw the cold death with dark, angry lines close together, but the bear only stared at them, uncomprehending.

How to describe the choking feeling, the terror?

She knew she would have to take him to the place and let him experience for himself what the cat man had left behind.

But not now. Not yet.

When the bear settled into his place near the opening, she was glad of it.

After a sleepless night, she led the bear back to the waterfall.

She had to stop now and then to let the bear catch up

with her, though normally they were much of the same pace. Her heart was beating so fast she felt it might fly away, and she slowed her pace only when she noticed an unnatural sting in the air.

The cold death had spread and encompassed more area now. She looked down to her paws to see that the ground itself seemed changed, even where the cold had not fully taken hold. The plants were not as green as they had been. They were tinged with brown and wilting, though there had been plenty of rain this spring.

It was worse closer to the stream, where the plants looked as if they had simply withered up and been blown away by wind. There was a gentle blanket of gray chaff everywhere, and all sign of life was gone.

The hound pointed to the stream and pantomimed the cat man reaching for the fish and knocking it against the rock. But that did not truly explain what she had seen. Frustrated, she tried once more to think.

But the bear did not wait for her. He moved a hind leg into the line of gray that marked the cold, then tottered and fell into it.

CHAPTER SIX

The Bear

THE BEAR COULD feel the cold seeping into his body, making his nose go numb at the tip as if there were snow falling outside and a wind howling deepest winter. But in a true change of seasons, he could still feel his heart beating, and the warmth at the core of his body. This unnatural cold made him disconnected from himself, as if his mind were no longer part of his bear's body but rising above it and watching with no feeling at all as it lay down and began to die.

The hound tugged at him from her place outside the line of full gray, but his body was a useless weight. At last she went into the stream and pulled at his bulk from there.

Immediately the water warmed him, chill as it was. There was a deeper warmth, of nature, that the water drew from other parts of the forest.

He and the hound rode the stream past all hint of

gray on the forest floor. About half the distance back to the cave, they fell on a bank and lay there, side by side, panting.

It was some time before the bear noticed the quiet. The animals were afraid of the cold death. But fear alone would not protect them if the cold death spread farther into the forest.

And he had no idea how it could be fought.

Perhaps there was one who did, but the thought of the wild man made the bear's jaw clench. He would not seek out that one willingly a second time.

Slowly he and the hound made their way back to the cave. He thought of how the death of that one section of the forest would affect it all. What of the insects that fed on the plants? The birds that fed on the insects? And those creatures that ate the birds?

It was almost too much to hold in his mind. He wished he weren't the least bit human, that he could not imagine how much worse things might become. But then he saw how the hound walked, slumped to one side, with no hope in her. She seemed to feel it exactly as he did.

So perhaps it had nothing to do with being human, after all.

They reached the crossover to the cave, and the bear stopped short. It was the scent of cold death that stopped him first, and then he realized there was something else. A figure standing in front of the cave.

A man, but not a man.

The bear remembered how the hound had tried to describe a man and a cat to him, and her shivering.

She tensed now and the bear could feel her ready to spring, to attack.

He roared and went forward himself, the hound close on his heels.

But the man-creature ran with a wild cat's speed and grace, leaping from stone to tree, and then from tree to tree without stopping.

The bear lost track long before he gave up the chase. The dark had aided the cat man, and the bear could see no farther than a paw in front of his eyes.

The hound whined at him, but he pushed her back toward the cave, toward home. Until they both felt the cold again.

Where the cat man had walked from the cave to the stream there was another barrier of gray and cold.

The cat man must have followed the hound's trail from the day before, but it was too dark to do anything now. They would have to wait until morning, near home but not in it. Perhaps never in it again.

He felt the hound quiver and moved closer to her. There was only the shelter of a small, budding tree nearby.

It was the longest night in the bear's memory, longer even than the first night he had spent as a bear.

He counted each heartbeat.

He had always thought he had found courage as

a bear. He had not realized that it was in part that he had had nothing to lose.

Suddenly he was struck with a flash of memory from when he was very young, when he ran too early into his parents' bedroom one morning, before his nursemaid could catch him.

He had caught them asleep, one of his father's arms wrapped around his mother's chest. His mother with one arm held up to catch his father's arm, as if to pull it closer to herself. Their legs entwined, the blankets thrown off, as if they did not need any warmth but what they shared with each other.

He had run away, out into the castle gardens. He had pouted there for most of the morning, missing breakfast. Then he had been dragged back to his bedroom for a nap that he was determined not to take.

He could only think about his parents and how they had been complete. Without him.

The first light of dawn stretched like fingers through the trees of the forest.

The hound woke and pulled away from him, then stood on all fours and watched as the sun reached the cave and its surroundings. What the cat man had done was starkly visible.

Just above the stream was the shelf of rock where the bear often came out during the spring or fall to let the gentle evening light fall on him as he dozed and thought of the past and what might have been. It had once had tiny fronds of fern growing up through cracks. These were gone, as if they had never been.

The bear swallowed hard before turning his gaze to the cave itself.

The cave was destroyed, the rocks collapsed, as if some living part deep inside had been torn away.

The bear felt his own legs fall out from under him. As he fell, he cut his face on a prickle bush by the stream, a bush he had always hated.

But now he wanted to sing to it, to praise it.

The prickle bush was still alive. It was green. It might yet survive. If so, it was the only thing that remained of his home that was as it had been for two hundred years.

He felt as wounded as if he had been cut through by a sword, and worse, for a physical wound could be healed. This—never.

CHAPTER SEVEN
The Hound

THE HOUND THOUGHT that they must go to Prince George. If there was any hope of fighting the cat man and his cold death, it would have to be with the prince. Yet he had used his great magic only once. Could he learn to control it? How much of the forest would be destroyed by that time?

She and the bear went to the edge of the forest near the castle. It had been months since their transformation, but still the hound was stung at the thought of how easily Marit had gone to a new life without her. Only at the wedding had she been acknowledged, and then with a tiny bow from Marit. Since then neither George nor Marit had come to visit in the forest.

The hound waited for some sign of a friendly face. She could not simply walk up to the castle door and scratch on it, howling for attention. She would be sent away.

At last she caught sight of a group of humans moving

toward the forest. The hound recognized George and Marit, along with a handful of others, most young and dressed as little more than peasants.

The hound noticed with some satisfaction that Marit wore practical trousers and a short jacket rather than the floating, gauzy thing she had worn at the wedding. But her face looked troubled.

From her bearing, the hound could see that Marit was bound to her prince and to those around him. These were her pack now.

The bear began to move toward the humans. The hound had to run to catch up with him.

The humans stopped at the edge of the forest, though the hound did not know why. There was no hint of the cold death here. Yet.

Then Prince George saw the bear. He started, then stretched out a hand.

"Bear, it has been too long," he said, and waved at the bear to come closer.

The other humans were wide-eyed at the sight of a huge bear approaching them, with the exception of one boy, who had very blond hair and a pinched face. He was utterly blank when he looked at the bear, as if he had never felt fear. Or had felt it too much and could feel it no longer.

"Where is—" said Marit suddenly.

And then the hound moved so that she could be seen. Marit threw her arms up and raced toward the hound, throwing herself to her knees and giving her a fierce embrace.

The hound stared at Marit, so tall and thin. Her red hair, once worn in the long style that her father and his kingdom expected of a noblewoman, was now cut very short. It stuck up all around her ears, but somehow it suited her. It made her look younger, and it fit the freckles that still dominated her face.

"We could not come. The danger of those who hate the animal magic is still so strong—we feared for you if we were seen to seek you," said Marit in a jumble of words. "We only dare to come into the forest here, at the very edge, and always we are careful to speak to different animals, so there is no pattern that can be seen by our enemies. Even so—" She stopped and turned to Prince George.

Gravely he said, "There has been more than one of those innocents we spoke to who have died. The burned body of one was left at the castle gate, as a clear warning to us. This has been the first chance we have had to come out into the forest in safety."

"Mar—" Marit started to say to the hound, then checked herself. "I don't know what to call you now."

The hound stared blankly. It had been the princess who had insisted on giving her a name. And after George loved her as a hound, she had taken that name for her own. It was confusing, if one cared about names. The hound did not.

Marit sighed. "'Hound' will have to do for now, I suppose. But how good it is to see you, truly. You look well."

The hound supposed it was true. She had more fresh meat now than she had had with the princess. And living in the forest gave her plenty of exercise.

"Ah, Bear," said Marit, stepping back. "It is good to see you, too." She put out a hand and touched the bear's back, then turned back to the hound.

"I must admit, being with you here makes me feel at home in a way that nothing else has." She took a breath and smiled ruefully. "Not even my own pillow, which George rode all the way to Sarrey to get for me when I mentioned to him once that I missed the smell of it. Three days he was gone, and used up two horses on the way. Just to get me a pillow. Can you imagine?" She shook her head and there was a hint of blush in her cheeks.

The hound remembered the possum the bear had brought to her when she was wounded and unable to move away from the cave herself. For her, too, it was a strange thing to be taken care of.

"Well, let's introduce them, shall we, George?" she said.

George bowed to her. He looked older and more self-assured, as much a man as a boy. As much a king as a prince, if only of this small part of his kingdom. His shirt was ragged and stained on the cuffs, and he seemed completely unaware of it. He had also put on some pounds around his chest and stomach—not all of it muscle.

"Sometimes I still do not believe my memories of that day, and my magic," said George. "It is good to see the truth before my face again."

The bear made a strange low sound.

Prince George moved gingerly closer to him. The bear's mouth gaped open, showing his huge, sharp teeth. George stared straight at them, then put his arms around the bear's shoulders and let his head rest there. Suddenly he seemed young again, hardly more than a boy.

He took a deep breath and pulled himself away.

"This is the bear and the hound I have told you about," he said, turning back to the others in the group.

Turning to the bear, George waved at the humans. "This is the school of magic."

The hound remembered George's enthusiasm for the school. But there were only a handful here. Was that all the success he had had?

Along with the blond-haired boy, there was a man with the tattoos on his face of a murderer from the southern kingdom of Thurat. One of the women was missing an eye and a hand, and her face had been burned terribly.

The hound wished she believed more in Marit's new pack's strength and loyalty. They did not hold close to her as they should, if the danger Marit and George spoke of was so constant.

"Well," said George awkwardly.

But the hound had no time to make him comfortable again. George might think his place threatened, but there was much worse to come, as he would know when she told him of the cold death.

"Our home is destroyed," she began, speaking in the language of the hounds.

"What?" said George, starting.

How many of the others understood her? Not the princess, nor from the looks of them the others. And the blond-haired boy seemed utterly uninterested. His whole body was turned away.

"The bear's cave, where we have lived since—since the transformation," she continued.

"But how was it done?" asked George. "There have been no earth rumblings, no lightning strikes. Other animals?"

Of a sort, thought the hound.

She looked toward the bear. She wished that he could tell his part of the story. The bear was far more experienced in magic than she was, and had more of the prince's trust. But the communication was left to her.

"It is a cat man," said the hound. She waited a moment to see how the prince would react.

"Cat man," he echoed.

The hound thought she saw a bit of movement from one of the other humans, but she was focused on the prince. "I think it is a cat, but it has been changed into a man. It brings a cold death with it that spreads through the forest," she said. It was the best she could do to explain.

"A cat man? I believe I have read an old, old tale of such a creature in this area. But it could not possibly be the same one after all this time, and so long away . . ." The prince trailed off.

"I do not know about your tale, but I know that this cat man takes life with pleasure. Soon the forest will be consumed."

George nodded. "I will do what I can with my magic. You have but to show me the way."

He turned back to Marit and the others. "You should go back to the castle. All of you. There is danger in this."

Marit grinned, a grin of defiance, of challenge. A hound's toothy grin, learned from her days in another form. "Is it to do with animal magic?" she asked.

"Yes," said George.

"Then we should go with you. What are we here for if not to learn about magic, dangerous or not?"

George shook his head. "No," he said, looking at her belly. "Not now."

And then the hound stared at Marit again. Her balance was different. And her smell. She should have noticed from the first. The princess was with child. Early still, not enough to show on her tall, thin frame, but it was there.

Yes, the prince would want to protect her.

But the princess would have none of it. "We are a school. If you protect us, we learn nothing."

The hound thought how a male hound would have reacted to his mate who refused to obey him. A cuff to the ear or a slash at the belly. More, if necessary.

But George was human, and so was the princess.

Far easier to be a hound, she thought. *Unless one is not a hound.*

George nodded slowly, almost imperceptibly. "You will come, then." He turned back to the hound and spoke to her quietly, under his breath. "The cat man—it is gone now, is it not? You only mean to show us what it left behind with its magic, yes?"

He was asking for the sake of the princess and the unborn child, not for himself.

"I think it has done its work here already," said the hound.

"Then take us," said the prince roughly.

The hound turned and led them, the bear following behind.

CHAPTER EIGHT

The Bear

COMING THIS WAY through the forest, they found further evidence of the harm done by the cat man. The bear could hear the voices of sick and dying animals calling out to him. He did not need to understand their languages to hear their pain and bewilderment.

But he watched Prince George and saw his pain. Each cry was like an arrow to his side. Princess Marit moved closer and then put an arm around him.

They reached the cave, and George tried to step past the stream into the area of cold death. Over and over again, George tried to force himself forward until he was retching on his hands and knees, his face pale and his breathing shallow and fast.

"Is there more?" he asked hoarsely.

The hound led George on to the place where the gray edge was seeping outward.

The humans moved slowly. The bear could hear their feet dragging through the dirt, and he and the hound had to stop many times to let the humans rest.

There seemed to be a taste of death in the air even some distance away, and the bear could see fallen animals scattered ahead, touched by enough of the cold to succumb to it, though the plants were not fully gray here.

The bear's breath came shallow and quick. This was his home. He had no kingdom anymore but this one, no castle but his cave. And for so long he had watched over this place, in his own way.

Now it was all disintegrating. Soon the remaining animals would be fleeing this forest and it would be deserted. The humans would encroach yet further here, and it would be as if this place, his place, never was.

"Oh," Prince George groaned, before they had even come within eyesight of the stream where the hound had seen the cat man, where the bear had first tasted the cold death, and where it was now fully black as ashes.

Princess Marit touched the prince's arm. "No need to go farther," she warned him.

George shook his head. Sweat streamed down his face. He struggled away from her and, bent over, moved forward.

The bear realized now that Marit might have known better than anyone why she would be needed here, though she had no magic of her own.

"Please!" she called after the prince. "Come back!"

George nearly tripped over a carcass.

Then, in horror, the bear saw it melting into the ground. Before his eyes, he could see the disintegration of one tiny squirrel's body as it became indistinguishable from the other bodies around it, falling into the gray deadness all around.

Surprised by the sudden change under his feet, George fell, landing flat on his face, his mouth touching the cold death.

"George!" cried Marit. She put out her arms and tried to press herself forward, into the worst of the cold death.

The bear pushed her out of the way and threw himself toward George.

Once he was there, however, he did not know how to get them both out. In the end, George stirred enough beneath him that the bear's contact with the ground was interrupted. The bear had just enough strength then to push George forward. Then George leaned back and tugged the bear out as well.

Once free, the bear felt numbness in his forelegs and -paws, and a point on his stomach that had had too much contact with the dead ground. George's lips were discolored, and one of his ears looked deflated.

Marit had to lead him in the right direction, away from the cold death, for he did not walk steadily now.

The hound walked at the bear's side.

When they had gone nearly to the other end of the forest, George stopped and called for food.

The blond-haired boy and one of the others brought out bread and dried fruit. George had it shared around equally, and offered some to the bear and the hound as well.

The bear ate a little, then turned to see that the hound, for all she had always turned her nose up at such meals before, also took a bit of the bread and chewed on it slowly. He thought she must be terribly hungry and afraid.

"I do not know how to battle this," said Prince George. "This pulls from me all that I am, all that I feel."

Was the prince giving up? The bear did not think him a coward, but had hoped for more.

"You are saying we must retreat and leave our dead behind?" asked Marit. The bear remembered her father was a warrior as well as a king. She would not be used to defeat.

"I am saying that it is one thing to cut a new channel for water that is already flowing. That changes only the course of the water, as I have done with you and the hound," said George. "But it is another thing again to fill a stream that has gone dry with water one must call from the sky to fall just so."

"And who could do this?" asked Marit.

"One who knows more of magic than I," said George. "One who breathes it in like a fish breathes water. One who has been part of magic from the first."

The bear felt a chill run through him, leaving a numbness in his paws. Who was the coward now?

"Let me tell you a story," said George. "It is a story about the wild man."

It was the last thing the bear wanted to hear. Had he not suffered enough at the hands of the wild man?

Yet for the sake of the forest animals and their magic, the bear was willing to listen even to this.

"It is a story of a challenge between the two greatest warriors: a man and a wolf. I had to read it through to the end before I understood how it had to do with the wild man.

"His name was Tors and he was a giant of a man," George said. "His legs were as thickly muscled as tree trunks and he could run as fast as a deer. He knew how to use a sword so well that no man dared stand against him, and he knew the minds of other men so well that he had never been surprised in battle.

"Tors had heard of the wolf known as the Bear-killer, who had killed a bear on his own when he was only two seasons old and then became leader of his pack. In the years following, the Bear-killer gathered more and more wolves to his pack until there were hundreds of them, a terrifying sight to see. So Tors went in search of the Bear-killer and found him with his pack.

"Using the language of the wolves, Tors challenged the Bear-killer to a race across the great globe itself, over mountains, rivers, deserts, snow, and oceans. This race would test endurance and determination as well as physical prowess and sheer ingenuity. It might take more than a year to finish, but the first of the two to return to the very place in the forest on which he now stood would be declared the winner. The other would lie down and give up his life for the first.

"The Bear-killer accepted the challenge. What else could he do? The human warrior had cried out to him in the hearing of his mate, his pups, and all the other wolves in his pack. And truly he wanted to fight the human. He was tired of the way in which humans saw the whole world as theirs. They cut trees and took over forests that belonged to the animals, and killed those who tried to fight for their homes. Humans were arrogant and had to be shown their true place, which was no higher than that of any other creature.

"'Then let it begin,' said Tors.

"'But wait!' called out the Bear-killer, for he was as cunning as the human warrior. 'Because you have set all the other conditions of this quest, I add this one: that those of our own kind who are able to help us shall be allowed to. Thus shall this test be more than for one man and one wolf, but for all men and all wolves.'

"Tors could not see that this would make any difference to the outcome of the race. The Bear-killer still had to run every mile of the race himself, as would he. So he agreed to this change, and the race began.

"Tors began to run toward the mountains in the east. The Bear-killer did the same. But a wolf runs faster than a man, so he was miles ahead before night fell. Then, in the dark, as Tors rested, the Bear-killer found another pack of wolves close by and spoke to them about the human warrior who believed himself superior to all wolves. The wolf pack was so incensed that they needed no suggestion from the Bear-killer as to what to do next. They attacked immediately, dozens of them coming in the dark against one man.

"Tors defended himself and killed them all. He cried out his triumph into the dark night so that the Bear-killer could hear that he had not beat the human warrior so easily. But Tors was wounded with many wolf bites and had to tend to himself through the night. In the morning he had not eaten well or slept, and when he began his journey again he was much weakened.

"He asked for help from other humans in villages that he passed through, telling them about his great quest to prove that a man is better than a wolf. They agreed that his quest was a good one, but they would not give him food unless he labored for it. So Tors was forced to stop for several days and was further delayed behind the Bear-killer. He told himself that the wolf, though moving well here in the mountains, would soon falter in the deserts.

"But there were desert wolves as well. And in each terrain that they passed through, the wolf never fell behind. Worse still, the human warrior became more battered as time went on, hungrier and thirstier and further in need of aid from the human villages he passed by. And yet they would give him nothing at all, or very little. They had excuses, for they said the harvest had gone badly, or the winter had been too cold. Tors drank from streams and ate raw meat, and made coverings for himself from leaves and grasses.

"But the wolf, the Bear-killer, was always treated kindly by other wolves, and they helped him in whatever way they could. They thought of any victory he would have against the human as their own victory, whereas the humans were too selfish to think this way. Tors was a man from another village, another kingdom, far away. If he won his contest, they would never know or care. So why should they share their resources with him?

"Tors began to see how selfish humans were compared to the wolves. It made him angry, and yet he wondered if he would have been any different if a stranger had passed through his village asking for help in a contest against an animal. For all his cunning and skill, Tors had never understood the world this way before. And he began to fear that he could lose this race.

"At last the two warriors reached the ocean. Staring out into it, seeing the human vessels that bobbed up and down in the waves, Tors felt he had found hope again. He turned to the Bear-killer and said, 'Are you ready to give up? If you tell me you are finished now, I will make your death easy.'

"The wolf spat at Tors and then leaped atop him and began to attack him in earnest, as he had never done before. It was a great battle, but it ended too soon, for a tidal wave washed over them and dragged them out to sea. Neither wolf nor man could survive alone in the terrible current. It was only in this intense moment of desperation that they reached for each other to survive. And in that moment when a man and a wolf tried to help each other instead of battle each other, they found the magic that binds humans to animals.

"And the two began to change into one.

"The man first grew the head of a wolf, and then the tail to keep him steady in the water. The wolf grew a man's long fingers for paddling. They pushed against the water to reach the surface. They kicked and swam as their lungs screamed. But it was not until they thrashed so violently that the two forms could no longer remain separate in one space. The two became one, and they were able to find air and breathe in life once more.

"A man and a wolf had gone into the water, but it was one creature that came out of it. This creature had wild eyes and a beard that was the grayish white of a wolf's skin. He no longer had the stature of a giant, but had something between the height of a man and a wolf. At times he could make himself into a wolf. At other times he took on only a few of the aspects of the wolf: the teeth, the claws, the tail. Often he looked simply like a very wild man, which he was indeed. A man who had become one with an animal and was happy with the change, and did not seek to return to the two separate creatures he had been."

The bear felt only a twinge of sympathy for the wild man. He, at least, had kept some of his human side. The bear had no such comfort.

George held up a hand. "There is more," he said. "The story I read insisted that the magic that bound the wild man into one form also bound him to life. When he is not found among those with the magic, he is to be found in the north, on the very highest peak of the sheerest mountains, where he watches over the magic still. Yet he is no servant of animal or man, but of magic itself, and he aids it always in the battle against unmagic," said George.

Unmagic. It was the perfect name for the cold death in the forest. Magic was a way of connecting with other lives. This—unmagic—was a way of severing all those connections.

CHAPTER NINE
The Hound

THE HOUND LOOKED at the bear. She had never seen him so curled into himself before. All because of the reminder of the wild man.

George leaned over Marit, then put a hand to her belly.

She whispered to him.

The hound thought of her own child, forever lost to her.

It was the way of the forest, a new generation rising to replace the old. Until the cold death had come.

Turning back, the hound caught sight of a flash of anger in the eyes of the blond boy. Suddenly he threw himself at George screaming, "Let the unmagic take you!" He kicked and punched at George until the bear pulled him off.

"I have protected you," said the prince. "Taught you. Fed you. Why would you attack me now?"

The boy spat out blood, uncowed. "You think I should be grateful?" he shouted at George. "That I should bow down to you as my prince in magic as well as kingdom?

"You do what you do for your own sake. You call us to this 'magic school' of yours so that you can make us your servants, harness our power to yours. You think that I cannot see through your schemes? I am not as stupid as they are." He waved behind him at the other humans, who flinched at his words.

"Why do you think there are so few of us here? A handful. That is not a hundredth of those who have the magic in a ten-mile circle around the castle, let alone in the whole kingdom. We all know what my father knew— that you will take what you can from us and leave us to die at the stake."

George opened his mouth as if to contradict the boy, then stopped himself. "Ah, that was your father," he said, his face going pale. "I am sorry for what happened to him. Truly I am. I wish I could have helped him."

Marit whispered, "No," as if she had done some evil herself.

The hound did not understand this human guilt the two felt, which stopped them from taking action against the boy.

He should be silenced, and permanently, whatever had happened to his father. He was a threat to Prince George, and his magic and kingdom.

But no one stopped his tirade. "You could have

judged him clean. You could have admitted to your animal magic then. But you turned your back on him and then listened to him cry out for help as he died in agony. And you waited to tell the truth about yourself until it was useful for you.

"I say that if this unmagic is a threat to you, well and good. Fight it alone. As my father said when he was burned, Prince George is no prince of ours. I will not be ruled by him. Not now and not ever!" He shook a fist and looked at the others.

The woman who had been burned spoke hoarsely. "Prince—" she began, then stopped. She looked back at the boy. "What do you say?" she demanded harshly.

"I . . . was a child," said George, eyes wet with tears. "I have regretted it all my life. I thought I would make up for it now."

The woman turned away from him.

The hound bristled at the disloyalty of what she had thought of as the prince's pack. They could fight him to show their anger. But to turn away was not houndlike at all.

Then the man with the tattoos came closer to George and the hound waited a moment too long, thinking that this was the way it should be done. A nip, a growl, and then all would be right again.

George held out a hand.

And was stabbed in the stomach with a knife that flickered out faster than the hound could follow. She thought as George stifled a cry how unfair it was that his own had used a weapon against him that he could not defend against—and without warning!

Humans!

The bear, stunned, stumbled forward and let loose the boy, who scrambled to his feet and laughed aloud. "To war!" he called. "We will bring down his kingdom and all those who hate magic in it. We are few, but we are strong!"

The hound leaped at the tattooed man, but he was already out of her immediate range.

She would have followed, but George called out, "Stop! They are my subjects. If anyone has failed, it is I who have not done enough to save—" He clutched at his stomach and his mouth made the last word soundlessly.

The hound could smell the flow of deep blood. Marit wept at his side, tore off her own jacket, and pressed it into the wound.

"You must get home, to the palace physician," she said urgently.

"If he doesn't also wish me dead," said George, a hint of a bitter smile on his lips.

"You idiot! Sometimes I could wish you dead myself," said Marit. She looked up at the bear and the hound as she helped George back toward the castle.

"I wish you well fighting the unmagic," she said. "But I cannot pledge any help to you now."

The hound barked her understanding. Prince George would defend magic on another front.

The bear and the hound would have to find the wild man, to see if he could help.

She looked at the bear, thinking how difficult it must be for him to face the man who had taken his human life from him.

Nonetheless, he found a branch and scratched in the ground with it.

The hound saw that he had drawn mountains and an arrow pointing north—to the wild man.

CHAPTER TEN

The Bear

THE UNMAGIC WAS in every part of the forest. There was no way of avoiding it and its effects completely. And, in fact, the bear felt compelled to witness as much as he could of the death of his forest and its creatures. It was his last gift to them, his last farewell.

He and the hound were silent as they walked side by side through the dry section of the forest, where the unmagic was at its worst. The bear walked all the way around the area, forcing himself to get as close as he could, to measure its size. It took several hours.

The forest was shaped like a coin that had been melted on one end, and it was on this end that the unmagic was strongest, though it permeated the whole forest. As he walked the edge, the fur on the back of the bear's neck rose and the hound whined.

The bear could see more than one mound of what had

once been an animal caught in the unmagic and unable to get out, as if pulled down into quicksand. Some of the mounds looked no more animal now than a pile of leaves, but the shape of them made the bear certain of what they were.

And then there were places where there were mounds next to mounds. Families of animals that had died together in the cold death, or perhaps one had died and then the others had died trying to save the first.

The bear had to stop then, to take a deep breath before he went on. He thought of the man he had been and the man he now was, despite the skin he wore. He gave grudging credit to the wild man for a portion of that change. He never would have suspected he could care so much for animals.

At the edge of the unmagic on one side, the bear stopped at a mound that for a moment had seemed alive. There had been movement there, he was sure. But now, when he looked again, there was nothing. He stared at it another moment, then turned away.

A sound pulled him back.

What was the mound? It was the shape and size of a deer, though the legs had been pulled into the graying ground. The outline of the head, turned too sharply to one side to be still alive, was fast fading, and the torso was long and thick.

Very thick, in fact.

Could it be two deer caught together?

Then, as he was watching, he saw the movement again, a faint beat coming through the skin at the top of the mound. The reality came clear to him in a stark moment. It had been a doe nearing her birthing time, and the fawn had been trapped inside of her. Now the unmagic that had killed the mother was burrowing deep into the tissues of her flesh to kill the babe.

The hound was suddenly at his side, whining.

It was the sound the doe herself might have made as her flesh sloughed off, knowing that she would never see her fawn's face, nor lick it free from the fluids of birth and watch it wobble on its new legs.

With a deep breath, the bear stood tall on his hind legs. He threw himself forward so that the weight of his body would carry him into the unmagic.

It was like falling into a frozen lake, as if the ice were shattering all around him and shards of frozen unmagic were slicing into him.

But he could hear the hound howling after him.

He dragged one paw forward toward the doe, sensing the life of the fawn beneath his claws. But it was fading. It would be gone if he did not act quickly.

He poured all of his energy, all of his own life, into one movement to press his claw into the abdomen of the doe.

It was not blood that spilled out, or any fluid that he recognized. It was the gray death itself, turned into a foaming gray gas that saturated his senses and made him choke for breath.

But when it had passed, he looked down and saw a hoof, then two.

The fawn seemed to have more strength than he did now.

It climbed out of the cavity of its mother's death and then faltered.

The hound leaped forward and tugged on the fawn's forelegs to get it moving away from its mother, away from the cold death.

The fawn took two steps forward, almost past the worst of the unmagic.

Then the hound somehow made her way to the edge of the unmagic herself and, barking, threatening, and dragging, pulled the fawn through to where there was green showing on the forest floor.

She looked over at the bear, her eyes so fierce that he knew she would try to come for him next. He would have to move if he did not wish her to endanger herself for him.

He bared his teeth and growled at her. Not much of a growl, perhaps, but it kept her back.

Then, inch by inch, he pulled himself forward.

After that it seemed easier. He lunged past the dark gray line of the unmagic and found himself face-to-face with the fawn. It blinked at him, utterly unaware that it should be terrified and shrink away from the bear who might devour it.

He turned to the hound and thought of how often he

had wished to die and had been unable to. Now he had never wished so much to live.

The hound helped the fawn on its way. It scampered deeper into the forest, away from the unmagic. Even so young a creature had the instinct to flee that if it could. But how long would the fawn last here, without a mother to protect and feed it? How soon would the unmagic spread to the whole forest?

Well, the bear would do what he could for it and for the other forest creatures, even if it meant facing the worst, the wild man.

The urgency with which the bear moved away from the forest was now hot and pressing. Night came and went, and still he kept on pushing himself, past Kendel, past Sarrey, into the north. The hound struggled to keep up with him and he thought only that it would be better for her to stay behind. He had no wish for her to meet the wild man and pay for mistakes she had not made.

Then, one evening, he could not see her or even hear her behind him. He had his first taste of what it was like to be without her. The loneliness clawed at his throat. Still, he forced himself on and told himself she would at least be safe without him.

But she caught up with him that night as he walked under the stars of a cooling summer sky. She was covered with dried sweat and her tongue fell out of her mouth as she panted. Her eyes were red and swollen and she moved as if one paw were lame.

His first feeling was a selfish pleasure at the sight of her.

And then he felt ashamed of himself. Had he not learned to care for others, to wish for what was best for them instead of for himself?

She looked at him, head to one side, and he lifted his head, turned his back to her, and kept on going.

It seemed the only way to protect her from the wild man and from magic ruining her life once more.

But the hound followed him and he could hear her struggle with her left hind leg, injured by the bears in the spring, dragging more and more.

He felt sick himself with the pace he had set, but he knew the hound must fall back before he could take any rest.

In time she would give up. He had only to keep at it.

Yet the hound did not rest. Despite her lame leg, she kept after him. At one point, as he stopped at a stream, she came up behind him and moved past him, not bothering to drink at all.

As if to prove that she could do whatever he could. And more.

Chapter Eleven
The Hound

IT HAD BEEN seven days of ruthless pace-setting by the bear. And still the hound kept at it, following him north to the wild man, dragging her wounded leg. She did not know why the bear was angry with her.

She was too stubborn to care. She only knew she would not let him beat her.

They had just entered a rocky forest in the foothills of mountains so large that they made the hound feel dizzy at the sight of them when the bear tottered and collapsed without a sound.

The hound slowed and approached him, sniffing. He smelled nearly as much like death as had the fawn they had rescued from her mother's womb. His fur was matted and his eyes were crusted shut.

She could see his chest moving evenly, however. He

had spent seven days without a full night's sleep, and he had not stopped to eat more than a few berries and roots and to drink from streams. She had taken down a large rabbit twice, and a field mouse several times, but the bear was relying on the wild man's magic to keep him going. In that sense, she supposed, it was a wonder he had lasted this long.

She was so tired. And now that she had the chance, she would not waste it with thinking. She felt all hound as she pressed her back against the bear's, almost as if they were back in the cave, and fell into the deepest sleep of her life.

When she awoke, it was with a start. It was bright daylight.

She had fallen asleep near dusk.

She could see ants and other creatures crawling on the bear, who was still asleep. And then looked to see them on herself.

She brushed them off, then carefully plucked them from the bear. She did not want him forced to awake before he was ready. His breathing was still very deep and regular, and he felt warm enough.

But when she pulled her body away from his, he stirred, then blinked at her, and shuddered.

The bear moved stiffly and slowly at first, making his way to a nearby pool of water. It was dark-colored, crusted over with moss, and it smelled ripe. But he drank it, and so did she. Her mouth was dry and her tongue thick after a night's rest—and more—without drink. Especially after the week that had preceded that night.

She thought she could sleep another day and night through if she were given the chance. But when she turned to look at the bear, she did not dare try to speak of it with him, even in her wordless way. He had that faraway look in his eyes again, and then he put his head down and began to move forward.

They walked until late afternoon, when the bear seemed to stumble with every step. The hound barked at the sight of some berries.

He tottered toward them. The bush was low enough that he had to lean to one side to reach them.

When he had finished eating, he looked a little better.

That was when the hound's eyes grazed over a rocky outcropping and saw a small pack of wild hounds, all gray except around their eyes, where their skin was white.

There were five of them, two larger than the others. Her mind instantly categorized them as lead male and lead female, but if that were so, why only three others? That was not nearly enough for a healthy pack.

Had they been attacked?

She saw no injuries on them.

She turned to look at the bear.

He saw the hounds as well. And was as curious about them as she was. Even in his current state, his eyes narrowed and took in every detail.

If there was an attack, thought the hound, it would be five against two—not good odds.

But the hounds did not attack.

They simply stared back at the bear and the hound. The largest, the lead male, even seemed to nod at the bear, as if they had met somewhere before.

The hound knew that the bear had traveled many places before he had settled in the forest near Prince George's castle. But that would have been long ago, before this hound could have been born.

So what was this?

The lead male turned back to the others and nodded at them in a way that seemed not at all houndlike. A lead male would bark and tell the others what to do in a commanding tone. Not guide them to do what he asked in a way that was considered polite only by humans.

Humans indeed. The hound looked again at the five. Two and three. This was not a pack, not even a small one.

This was a family.

And since there were no families of hounds that she had ever heard of, she could only draw one conclusion: they were not hounds.

They wore the bodies of hounds, but that was all.

As they came closer, the hound became more certain of her suspicion.

They did not smell like hounds. They did not move or speak like hounds.

And they did not look at the hound or the bear as one animal looks at another.

Suddenly all her questions seemed answered as the animals transformed before her very eyes. The five hounds became humans, one after another.

A man and a woman, and three children: two girls and a boy, the youngest of all, perhaps five years old.

"We show ourselves to you. Then you show yourselves to us," said the man. He had an old, puckered scar that ran the length of his face.

The bear shook his head in a clear negative.

The scarred man set his jaw and took a step forward. "How shall I know that you are not sent to destroy us unless you also show me your magic?" he said in a dark tone.

The hound made a whining sound.

The man stepped closer, and when the bear went down on all fours in a show of submission he put a hand on the bear's shoulder. The man closed his eyes, then nodded.

"Ah, I see."

What did he see? He certainly did not speak to the bear as he would to another animal. Nor did he look at the hound that way.

"Come, then. I am Frant and my woman is Sharla. We will welcome you with such as we have." His gesture included the hound as well.

The hound found herself warmed by the family's ease in the presence of animals. She would never have suspected that she could be with humans again and not feel discomfort.

But these humans did not live in a castle and wear foolishly uncomfortable clothing. They did not seem to have ridiculous rules and lists of names and polite words to offer as they stabbed one another in the back.

It was almost like being in a pack again.

And yet she would not say that they acted like hounds would, either. No hounds would accept two strange animals into their pack, even if they were not afraid of the damage they might do.

The hound wondered if perhaps she had changed a little as well.

All of them moved together back toward the rocky outcropping.

After a few steps, the hound noticed that the boy changed back into a hound.

Then the female, Sharla, shook her head at him sternly and he took the shape of a boy once more. The boy was more comfortable in his hound form than his human one, it seemed. The girls were more obedient, but the hound suspected they felt as the boy did—that they belonged in the forest, with the animals, more than in a village with other humans.

They found a copse ahead, and there Sharla prepared a varied meal. There were roots and berries to satisfy the bear, but also plenty of meat for the hound.

The hound thought that the animal was fresh killed,

but she noticed that it was an old one, and that one of its legs was withered. A mercy killing?

It was tough, but better than nothing at all. At least the taste of the blood was fresh, and the meat was not cooked.

She noticed that one of the girls and the boy ate more of the meat than either of the parents and the other girl. And the bear, of course, ate only the roots and berries.

For her part, the hound ate meat, but not as much as she would have liked. She was used to gorging on a feast, and then going without for days on end. But such were the compromises to be made with humans.

The fire was not large, as a human might make. It was just enough to cook a few roots and then Sharla kicked it over and buried it. No fire kept for light and the feeling of protection against the strange creatures of the forest, as humans would do.

After that there were only stars above for light, and the hound noticed that there were no animals anywhere near them, as far as she could see—or smell. They kept their distance, as if they could tell that they did not belong amid this magic.

But the hound, for the first time since she had been touched by the magic that made her human, felt as if she did truly belong among others.

Chapter Twelve

The Bear

AFTER THE SPARSE meal was eaten, the bear allowed himself to put his foreboding about the wild man out of his mind. He was glad for a chance to rest at last. The gift of long life from magic did not mean boundless energy. And he hoped to learn much from these humans.

Their magic was more powerful than anything the bear had heard of, in his own time or in Prince George's, but in addition to that, the bear felt enormous gratitude for the way these humans treated the hound. Even George and Marit did not see her as these people did. The princess had treated the hound like a hound, a wild creature. And she was that—but she was more, too. No one but this family had seen that as the bear did.

The sun faded in the sky and the stars came up. It was a warm night with a gentle wind. The bear remembered many a night like this that he had spent in his castle, watching others dancing and drinking himself to oblivion. He had awoken only to vomit into the wind, stare at the stars once, and go back to sleep.

He was a bear now, but how much happier he was here.

With the hound.

Frant spoke then, as if he had been steeling himself to offer this much of himself. It was the first time he had seemed to struggle, and when he spoke it was of magic—and his past.

The bear was glad that he understood, though he could not speak in return. The details of the story were very different from his own, but somehow the way the man spoke of it, it seemed much the same.

"My father was always proud of his magic, and though he did not speak of it openly, he and my mother taught me well," Frant said. "Until—"

He struggled, then went on: "They were both killed when I was nine years old. A neighbor had come to warn them of the imminent attack, but by then the mob was too close behind. To save me, they sacrificed themselves and sent me to safety with him."

A man daring enough to save a boy with the animal magic was surely a courageous one, thought the bear.

But Frant's expression twisted with pain. "He left me alone in the woods, and told me never to return anywhere near my home or his. He said that if I did, he would be the first to light the match to my bonfire."

All sympathy had gone, and the bear felt a low growl rise in his throat for this man who had pretended to help, then had abandoned a small boy to his lonely fate.

Frant nodded, as if he had been asked a question. "I have thought about it in the many years since then and I believe I understand now what he did. This neighbor lived on a farm adjoining ours. I think he hoped to claim my parents' farm for himself. When they were dead, he had to make sure I could not gainsay him."

There was no forgiveness in Frant's voice.

"He saved your life," said Sharla softly. "I must be forever grateful to him for that."

"Only because it was easier to frighten a child than to kill him," said Frant. "I owe him nothing for that." He stared at his wife until she looked away. "I was left to raise myself. For many years I lived with the animals. Sometimes as an animal, sometimes as a boy. But soon I became lonely and I began to seek out others like myself—with the animal magic." He nodded at his wife.

The bear stared at her, seeing both hound and human in her. But it was the human that stood out. What animal would have compassion for the one who threatened her mate? Not his hound, he did not think.

Sharla said, "My story is simpler. I did not discover who—and what—I was until I was nearly fourteen. My parents were horrified, and I woke one night to hear them discussing how they might kill me to prevent the stain on their reputation. I fled north as an animal, thinking I would never see another human all my life. And then I met Frant, not far from this very place." She was finished, that quickly.

And again the bear was reminded of the hound. She found language of different sorts useful, but she did not indulge in idle chatter.

Frant said, "We have lived like this for most of our lives now. We are used to it and would not change for our own sakes. But we worry for our children. They have only each other for company and know nothing of human ways."

"They are happy enough," said Sharla. "And human ways are not necessarily better than animal ways."

The bear pondered this. He respected animals, cared for them, honored them. But given a choice, he would not choose to remain as a bear. Yet this family had grown used to both forms.

"Perhaps," said Frant. "But still, there are things that I would like to see made possible for them. They have never seen a book. Or a dance. Or a well-baked loaf of bread. And more than that—I worry for their futures."

The bear ached at this thought. He had not known how much he wanted a child until he realized he would never have one. A bear cub would never be a substitute, for it would only remind him of all that it was not.

"We must be patient," said Sharla confidently. "There are others like us. You see, these two are proof of it. In time we will find more. And then our children will be well matched in marriage."

"And if not?" asked Frant, as the bear would have asked himself.

A flicker of pain crossed her face, but then Sharla spread out her hands. "They spend their lives as animals. They live with animals. They speak as animals. Perhaps it would not be so bad if they loved as animals."

Frant spat. "They are humans."

"And does that mean that they are above the animals?" asked Sharla.

"Yes!" said Frant fiercely.

The bear thought of the hound. He did not think himself above her, and yet there was a barrier between them, despite all they shared.

Sharla turned to her oldest daughter and said, "Tell the story of the boy who was raised by wolves."

The girl told the story easily, as if she had heard it many times before.

"Once there was a boy whose mother was killed by wolves. But the babe she carried on her back they took back to their den with them. Perhaps they meant to eat him at first, for he made such a terrible noise.

"But when the lead bitch saw the tiny boy, she offered him her nipple to suckle on, for she had only the day before lost her own son. And while this boy was hairless and moved like a worm, still he was better than nothing. He was warm to snug up against and he eased the ache of her full breasts. And his face was expressive, for when he cried he was as sad as any creature she had ever seen, but when he suckled from her he was perfectly still and content. And when she played with him, he laughed as loud as the birds in the sky.

"She became quite fond of him, though his teeth were weak and he could not run on all four limbs like the other wolves. In time she began to think of him as her own son. She forgot that he had been brought to her as an infant, the dead child of a woman they had killed and devoured. She thought of him as a wolf, smart but weak."

The girl telling the story looked at her brother for a long moment, then hurried on.

"But the day came that hunters came through the forest, and the boy was discovered with the wolves. The hunters killed two of his packmates, then brought the boy down with them and carried him back to the human dens beyond the forest. The bitch wolf who had been the boy's mother said farewell to him in her heart and did not think to see him again.

"Until the boy returned. This time he was clothed as a human, and he strode on two feet as he had first learned, before the wolves had taught him better. He smelled as a human smelled, yet he spoke in the language of the wolves.

"The bitch wolf ran from him, but he ran faster and

farther. When he caught her, she trembled in his arms.

"'Mother,' he called her.

"And he brought her home to his new human den, to honor her."

The bear shuddered.

"Of course, the mother wolf was uncomfortable there," said the girl. "She could not bear the smell of the smoke or the taste of cooked flesh. She hated the way her once-wolf son looked, in his human clothes. And the soft touch of the furs under her feet here seemed wrong, for there was no contrast of hard ground underneath. She whined and whined at him until he let her go.

"He mourned her absence, but in time taught his own son to speak the language of the wolves as he had learned it. They went often to the forest and called to the wolves, and though his wolf-mother was long dead, still the wolves knew him and did not fear him. They spoke to him freely, and his son learned in his turn the way to speak with wolves. And with other animals.

"At the end of his life, the man went to the forest and lay down, calling to the wolves to come and devour him. But as the wolves came closer and began to tear at him, the man's body was transformed into the body of a wolf. He died as a wolf, at their hands, and this, they say, was the beginning of the animal magic."

The bear thought of the magic he had seen in Prince George's kingdom—of speaking to animals only, not transforming into them. What had happened? Even Prince George had never made himself into an animal. Was magic growing weaker with time?

"Good," said Sharla to her daughter. "You always tell that story with feeling."

"And what is your point?" asked Frant. "That those who have grown up too much with animals have no chance of being happy with humans?" He glanced at his son and then away.

"No," said Sharla gently. "Only that there is animal in all of us, and the more we have of it, the more magic we have. We should seek it out, for it is that which makes us truly alive."

Frant's jaw was clenched. "I want my son to have a life like mine."

"And if he wants one that is better for him?" asked Sharla.

She suddenly shouted at her daughters to leave their brother alone, speaking partly in human language and partly in the language of the hounds. Annoyed with their teasing, the boy had begun biting his sisters as a hound would have done.

Finally the others quieted and slept.

But the bear stared at the stars, thinking of the approaching encounter with the wild man. He did not know what would happen this time, but he knew what had happened last time. The wild man had been harsh and unrelenting, hardly human at all. He had been a mouthpiece for the magic.

The bear feared that magic greatly. But he feared the unmagic even more.

His thoughts turned to the hound.

He had allowed her to come too far with him. He could have stopped her and he had not.

Now he would.

Chapter Thirteen

The Hound

IN THE MORNING the hound awoke as the family prepared to leave. The bear was still sleeping, and she thought she should leave him be.

The boy spoke in the language of the hounds, furtively watching for his mother's disapproval. He was in the shape of a boy, and the others of his family all spoke as humans.

But the hound loved to hear the familiar sounds, and to be able to speak back in them was too tempting for her to resist.

She listened as he told her of the best parts of the forest here for hunting, for hearing howls echoed back, for running a race without obstacles. He wanted her to race with him and changed himself into a hound to do so, but his mother called him back and insisted he help with the chores around the camp, such as disguising their tracks and scattering dirt over the fire and their sleeping places to make sure no smell of them remained.

Just before they left, the hound had an idea. Speaking to the boy had made her realize that she could speak to the family as well. They would understand her.

Excitedly she leaped toward the woman and explained about Prince George and his proclamation about animal magic. She told them about his history with magic, his mother, and his school for animal magic.

Frant's eyes lit, but he was cautious. "And can he protect us?" he asked, in the language of the hounds.

The hound thought of the blond boy and his call for war. Still, if there was ever a hope for the family to find safety in using their magic freely, it was with George.

"With his own life and the power of his kingdom," said the hound firmly. "He will do all he can." She would have sworn it if there were words for such a thing in the language of the hounds. But it was a human thing.

Sharla asked, in the language of humans, "He has the magic himself?"

The hound nodded.

"How do we know he will not be murdered and all the rest of us with him?" asked Frant.

The hound did not know how to answer that. Hounds expected death. Humans found it a surprise, as if life could exist without death alongside it, as if all death were the death of unmagic.

"If we wish to have a home, we must take a risk," said Sharla. "Why not with this man, at this time?"

"Risk our children?" asked Frant.

"They are at risk in any case. The only difference is that with the prince the reward is greater."

Frant thought a long time, then nodded.

"Thank you," said Sharla, tears in her eyes, and for the first time speaking in the language of the hounds. "And thank him as well." She gestured to the sleeping bear.

When the bear awoke at last, the family was long gone, along with all traces of their presence.

The hound waited for him to stretch and find a morning drink before she tried to tell him where the family had gone. She noticed that the bear seemed unusually quiet and his expression was dark and distant. She thought it was only that the family was gone, and he was lonely again for human company.

But when she turned at the sound of his approaching, he was a great blur of movement rushing at her face. She had no chance to cry out, or to think at all, before he slammed into her side with his head.

In the long moment of her falling, she searched for some explanation, and knew that was a human thing. A hound needed no reason for violence in the forest.

Then she felt the pain, the lack of breath, the ground driving into her chest. She was a hound again. In a battle with a bear.

She slowly pulled herself up, her legs running cold with sweat, but she did not try to escape. A hound would never turn away from a battle.

The bear snarled at her, then came running once more. This time he did not charge into her and send her flying. He let his claws slash into her belly.

She threw herself at the bear and fought for her life. She bit and clawed and kicked and tore, and then stopped suddenly as the pain reached her with a sharp burning sensation. It was too much. Her eyes glazed over and her body slowed. She waited for death, as any hound would wait, panting, gasping, wheezing.

And saw the bear's face over hers, grief and disgust in his eyes.

And she remembered moments together with him, in the cave, in the forest, with the cat man.

She reached out a paw to offer him comfort.

And the bear lifted her into the air and threw her backward. She could feel the bite of the wound in her side. Then the tree behind her struck like a sword.

She could see nothing.

But she could smell the bear near her, hovering again.

She opened her mouth, wanting to say one last thing to the bear, but then she remembered that he could not understand her.

He would never understand her.

She woke in the dark, sprawled on the forest floor, her mouth filled with blood and leaves, and the bear nowhere in sight—or smell.

A sensible hound would lie there until recovered. Or bark softly, hoping for other hounds of her pack to hear. Or drag herself away from the site of the battle.

She did none of those things.

She thought of the bear's disgusted expression before he had thrown her away from him.

It only made sense to her when she took the time to puzzle it out, as a human would.

She knew the bear was afraid of seeing the wild man again. She thought that he must be protecting her in his strange, human way.

Stupid man.

Did he not see that there was strength in pack, no matter how small it was?

She tested her legs separately before she tried to put any weight on them. Her lame leg, the left hind leg, had taken the worst of the fall. It was very sore and swollen, but not broken. The others were well enough—she could put weight on them without sharp, stabbing pain.

She tested herself further.

When she shifted, she could feel the tightness on her belly where the bear's claw had caught her. The wound had already begun to heal, but the scab of dried blood was tight. She would tear it open if she tried to move. More if she tried to walk or run. But that did not matter.

The hound crawled forward, feeling weak and unsteady. Her vision swam. She had eaten the evening before the bear attacked her, but how long had it been since then? If she were to recover from this, she needed strength, and that meant food.

She looked around her and saw beetles boring into a fallen log. A hound did not eat beetles.

But in an emergency a human would.

She put out a paw, scooped up a handful of beetles, and poured them into her mouth.

She swallowed as quickly as she could without chewing. Nonetheless, her stomach felt tight and hot, as if the beetles were not yet dead and were running around inside of her.

She waited, and gradually felt better.

More beetles?

No.

She pulled herself up on all fours and limped, tail between her legs, head close to the ground to sniff for water.

There was a pond ahead, fed from an underground stream she could smell but not see. It was not deep, but it was enough for her to drink from, and the water was fresh.

She slaked her thirst, and strangely felt even more hungry.

It bothered her that she could not ignore her hunger.

But when an animal was hungry, it acted on that hunger. Only a human tried not to feel what she felt.

For now, she would do as a hound and deal with her hunger.

She waited by the stream. It was a good place to be, for other animals must come here.

Soon enough, a vole stopped to get a drink.

She pounced on it and killed it instantly. She would ordinarily have taken her time to enjoy the taste of it, but she found herself hurrying through the meal as only a human would, for all that mattered was filling her stomach enough to follow the bear.

She washed herself in the stream, cleaning the dried blood off her belly.

She went back to where she had last seen the bear, set her nose to the ground to find the bear's scent, and there it was—headed directly north.

The hound followed the scent for a full day before she allowed herself to rest for a few hours the next night. The mountains were growing steeper here. She had to stop frequently to catch her breath, and she left a trail of blood drops behind her. Her belly wound had reopened and oozed blood down her left hind leg, but it closed again as she rested.

She went another day, and found a place where the bear had fallen. She could smell his scent, and then suddenly it was gone. She had to go back down to another level to find it again, at a less steep section of the mountain.

She saw berry bushes now and again that the bear appeared to have picked from, but no roots. He seemed to sleep near rocks, as if to make a place like his cool cave.

The hound slept near logs, with her back to them. A part of her was afraid that the bear would come back and fight her again, so she prepared for that possibility. She was ready for a fight at any moment, waking or sleeping, climbing or resting.

In two more days the hound was over the first mountain range and got her first glimpse of the larger mountains beyond. She had never seen anything so impressive.

King Helm's palace with its stone towers and guards was merely a poor imitation of this beauty. The mountains rose up so sharply that anyone would look at them and tremble.

Stopping there, the hound felt the magic.

She had felt something before, a pressure inside her head, a feeling of heaviness. But she had not been sure what it was. She thought it might simply be the effect of the mountains themselves, how high they were.

Or it could have been the exhaustion she felt, and the sense of loss, after the bear had left her and she had to travel alone through a place she had never seen before.

But as it continued, she realized it was none of those things.

It was a magic so immense and powerful that it could fill the open space of the mountainous expanse and still throb and pulse at her, as if demanding that it spread yet farther.

Prince George's magic, when it had transformed her

back into a hound, had been a kind magic. It had not been painless, but it had touched her with no intent except to do what she most wished for. It was an obedient magic, meant to be called for and used.

This magic was its own wild thing, as much like the magic she had felt before as was a trained pup to a wild hound.

For a long moment she faltered.

She could go back, she thought.

To the forest at the foot of the first mountains.

Stay there, be safe. Wait for the bear to return.

But she had never been a coward, not as a wild hound and not as a human princess, either.

The bear belonged with her, and she would go to him and face what he would face.

She moved onward, her face against the magic as if against a strong wind.

Chapter Fourteen
The Bear

THE BEAR HATED the wild man's mountains. He hated the small rocks that tore at the soft spots on his paws and the large rocks that cut at his skin when he squeezed by them. He hated the way that the rocks shifted as he stepped on them, then heaved him forward to knock him down, breathless and bruised.

He hated the thin air that made it so that he had to take in two breaths for every step he took and still feel as though his lungs were constricted. He hated the cold that the wind whipped at him when he was sharp and awake, but he hated it just as much when he was trying to rest, and the cold, persistent and prickling, kept at him.

Most of all, though, he hated the pressure of the magic on every part of him, overwhelming and unrelenting.

How to describe it?

A fine meal at court, when he had been king and dish after dish had been brought before him, each more delicious than the last. His stomach was full early on, but he could not stop taking just one more bite, and another bite.

It had nothing to do with not offending his cook. He was king. He could do what he pleased, and the cook had no say in it.

It was only that he wanted more.

This magic was like that. Some part of him wanted it, though another part of him was overwhelmed by it.

He felt overcome by the sweet scent of the brush here. He felt even the tiny thorns in his paws from the little creeping vine that seemed to find a place to grow even in the deepest crevices of the rock. For it was as if the vine spoke to him and the brush sang to him. They knew themselves and they knew him.

He had no doubt that this was where the wild man must be. Who else could survive here?

His dread rose as it began to snow. Soon he could no longer feel his extremities. And at every step he was afraid.

He remembered a story he had heard once, of a man who had decided one day to change himself into a snake because it was the least like himself of all the animals. A snake had no legs, had scales, and was not a warm-blooded creature. So becoming a snake would prove that he had more animal magic than any pretenders.

But when the man became a snake, he was so interested in his new body, in turning this way and that, in discovering how quickly he could move and how food would taste when swallowed whole, he lost all sense of his human self.

He died when he tried to attack a human—one of his own friends, in fact, who had come in search of him. But the friend had reacted automatically to the danger of poison from the snake and used a hunting knife to pin the snake to the floor of the forest, then his feet to stomp the life out of it.

As the friend held the dead snake in his hands, he realized his mistake at last. But he did not weep.

"It is better thus," he said. "For a man who forgets himself is better dead."

The bear fought to not forget himself amid this great magic.

He had been King Richon.

He had been turned into a bear by the wild man.

He had left the hound behind, had hurt her when she did not deserve it. But he would have done it all over again if he had to, to save her from this magic that battered him even now—and would get worse.

He pulled himself up to another shelf, using a boulder to his right for leverage. As he tottered, the boulder slipped from his grasp and fell off the cliff. Its fall took several long seconds. The bear did not look down.

He thought how dangerous this journey would have been with the hound.

He took a rest for two breaths, then heard a sound behind him, a scraping.

He turned and craned his head to look down, but he could see nothing. The snow was falling more heavily now, and it made everything indistinct.

Perhaps the wind had blown a small rock, and that was what he had heard.

He was no longer sure of himself. His limbs felt heavy and swollen. He was so tired that he spent much of the time moving forward with his eyes closed, as if half in sleep.

He went on for several more hours, hearing nothing.

The journey was excruciatingly slow. The climb was so sheer that he had taken only a few steps before there was another sheer cliff before him that he had to scale. He forced himself to go onward. If he stopped now, in this snowstorm, he could freeze to death.

But he felt so much warmer when he stopped.

He awoke, startled, and did not know how much time had passed. He could see nothing. Was it night or had the snowstorm become blinding?

His eyelashes had frozen shut. He rubbed at his eyes. Then opened them again.

There was a little light now.

But he still did not know how long he had slept.

And then he heard another sound.

It came from below him, but when he slid closer to the edge to look over, he swayed and nearly fell over.

He crawled back and listened again.

94

It was not the wind. It was too persistent a sound, too patterned.

Silence, scraping, scraping, silence, scraping, scraping again.

The same sounds the bear himself would have been making if he had been climbing.

Was any predator so desperate as to chase the bear up these cliffs?

He listened again.

There was breathing as well, heavy, gasping breaths, as if from a creature in pain.

It took a long moment before the bear realized that he recognized the register of those breaths.

It was a hound.

His hound.

"No!" The bear bellowed, a mournful cry that stopped the sound of scraping below him. But not for long.

When it began again, he could only think that he must get to the top first, enter the wild man's lair and finish his business before the hound reached him.

He could not fight her here. It would be her death. His, too, most likely, but it was her life he had wanted to preserve. He had been willing to do anything for that, even make her hate him.

And now it seemed she had been more stubborn even than he had imagined.

He forced himself to climb again, to match his

movements with hers, and then to exceed them. He gave himself no respite. This was a competition of speed and dexterity rather than sheer strength. The bear did not know if he would win.

At last he could see no cliff directly in front of him. He stumbled forward, hands outstretched to feel for the edge in case the snow had obscured it.

But this was level ground.

And the snow had lightened up enough that he could see.

There was a long stone shelf here and below him he could see the mountains in a circle, as if this peak were the jewel set in a crown, and extending out from that first circle was another circle, and another.

He could only see the faintest glimpse of the lowlands that he had come from and the forest beyond that.

The wind had quieted.

And still the bear could not hear the sound of the hound climbing behind him.

Was it only a matter of minutes before she arrived?

Or had she fallen?

He could not tolerate that thought.

Perhaps she was resting for a moment.

He had to get to the wild man now. The bear tried to call out and was infuriated by his limitations as never before!

He saw a pine tree ahead and moved toward it.

The closer he got, the more he realized that this

was no ordinary tree. It had been trained to grow tight around the edges, with the branches making walls, and one opening left so that there was a glimpse of the openness inside.

He stepped to the opening in the tree and bent down to enter, but the tree rose up to accommodate his height. The whole thing moved, as if it were alive.

The bear swallowed hard and concentrated on the scrapes and cuts on his body. It took away a bit of the fear of seeing the wild man again.

This was what he had come for, but it was like becoming the boy king again, with so little experience, too much pride, and no magic at all.

Then he heard movement behind him and turned to see—

The hound.

She was covered in snow and blood and dirt, hardly recognizable from the graceful creature she had once been.

She stared at him, as if waiting to see if he would attack her again.

But it was too late now. She was here. There was no protecting her from the magic of the wild man or anything else.

He thought for a moment about what the journey might have been like if they had been together, helping each other, comforting each other. It was a painful thought, and he pushed it away.

The hound barked once roughly, and the bear could hear her pain in it.

He opened his mouth and let out a sound in return, one that expressed his grief and his sudden, overwhelming happiness at seeing her alive.

He had always tried not to speak in front of the hound before, because it was embarrassing to him to make sounds that had no meaning. Now his pride was stripped away.

He stared at her wounds. He could still see the streaks of red where he had cut into her belly, a wound that might have been healed by now if she had not come after him.

He could see the way she limped on her left hind leg. He could tell by the way she shifted her weight that there were bruises beneath her dark skin.

All his fault.

CHAPTER FIFTEEN
The Hound

THE HOUND SAW the wild man standing behind the bear and gaped.

He was wild indeed, with hair down to his chest in front, dark in spots but gray in others, and a grizzled beard. He wore nothing at all, as a wolf would, but somehow he wore it with a human confidence. He was not large, certainly not when compared to the bear. He was a little taller than the princess, but wiry thin. There were many old scars on his body.

She had heard of the wild man in the human stories of the bear's transformation.

She thought she would fear him, but she felt for him much as she did for the strange tree he stood beside, which seemed to open its branches to invite them in. Such a tree could not have grown without magic, and the magic seemed to add to it rather than make it less than it was. So it was with the wild man.

He gestured for them to move into the shelter of the tree. It was not warm inside, but it was not cold, either.

"Well come," said the wild man, holding out his hand. He spoke to the hound first, and she trembled a little at the way his voice penetrated directly to her mind rather than through her ears.

He turned to the bear. "And you, well come. It has been some years, has it not?"

The bear was careful to step inside the tree and move to the side, all without touching the wild man.

The hound, however, held out her front right paw and shook the wild man's hand. She had not done it with another human before because she had felt it would make her less of a hound. But with the wild man that didn't seem possible.

He spoke in a language that was pure magic, not hound and not bear and not human.

"You must eat with me," said the wild man, and he gestured to a short table with flat pillows around it, perfectly situated for a hound or another creature who came to eat with the wild man. Or a human.

The bear lumbered forward and sniffed at the bread he was offered. He seemed to eat it only reluctantly—as if afraid of what the wild man might have put in it.

As for the hound, she ate the bread without hesitation, but was surprised to discover that it tasted exactly like the best killing she had ever made. It was fresh and salty, and she felt as though somehow the bread were dripping blood down the back of her throat.

After they had filled their starving bellies, the hound looked up at the wild man and spoke to him in the bear's place, for she knew he could only speak in groans and growls.

"We come to ask about a creature we have seen, a cat man," she said, intending to speak in the language of the hounds, though when it came out it sounded different than before, and she could see from the bear's attitude that he could understand her.

The wild man's magic must have made it possible, just as it made it possible for him to be understood by all.

The wild man nodded, as if not truly surprised. He would know the tale of the cat man, of course. "And what does it do, this cat man that you have seen?" he asked cautiously.

"It destroys life. It sucks it from the earth and leaves nothing behind. It is not even like death," said the hound, struggling with the limitations of a hound's language even here. "It is a coldness that the forest has never seen before, for death there always brings forth another life. And this brings nothing."

The wild man nodded. "Unmagic," he said.

"Yes," said the hound softly. She prepared herself to receive some terrible magic once more, to help the forest.

But the wild man sighed. "There are many stories of the beginning of magic, but not so many of its end. Some say that the beginning is the birth of the first twin and the ending the birth of a second. All that happens between the two is the agony of a mother waiting for relief.

"Others tell that time itself is a lover's chase that seems long to those who are running but to others is but a moment that is drawn out until the anticipation is over and the lovers united. When the lovers, who are magic and unmagic, fully embrace, they will cause a conflagration that will destroy each other and all other living things.

"It has been my task to hold off this final destruction. It is an eternal battle, without hope for peace. For the end of magic cannot be bargained with or bribed. It presses forward, relentless and unendingly powerful. But still I fight it.

"Because while I cannot stop it entirely, I can delay it. With each victory I hold back the power of the unmagic to allow magic for another year, or another century, or two centuries to allow more children to find the happiness that only comes from the play of magic in the forest, more animals to see humans not as enemy but as kin.

"Yet I find myself growing weak."

The hound could not believe it. The wild man held more strength than she had ever felt. She thought of what he might have been before now and had a glimpse of why the bear had feared him so.

But if he could not help them, then this journey had been useless.

"It is not time for the magic to end," the wild man

continued. "So while I no longer have the strength to leave this place and go to do the work of magic out there"—the wild man waved behind them, down the mountain—"I can still bring those who are necessary to me and use them to help me gain another decade—or more." He stared hard at the hound.

The hound was frozen, but the bear moved between her and the wild man. She was grateful for his attempt at protection, though she doubted he could stop the wild man from doing what he wished to her.

The wild man's voice spun out like steam under the boughs of an oak. "I once worked within the fabric of time, moving forward, always forward, as it does. But I do so no longer. To save magic, I shift between times. I tinker here and there, then step back and see what else must be done. Always to save the magic.

"So it was that when I came to you, King Richon—"

The bear stiffened at the mention of his old name, as if touched by old wounds.

The wild man took a breath. "To stave off the power of the unmagic, I had to make you live another life. You had to cease being a king and become instead one of the creatures that suffered by your mistreatment. You had to feel the need for the magic that holds humans and animals together, and that took many years.

"Yet your kingdom needs you to return, so I held time open for you to go back and be king once more. If you so choose."

The hound's head ached.

So the bear was to return to his kingdom in the past, to find the unmagic and stop it there. But what of her?

The bear moved to her side, but it seemed she needed no protection from the wild man's magic, after all.

"I can send you back in the form of the man you were," said the wild man. "Once there, you must choose again to aid the magic. If you fail, I will be forced to find others who may mend the damage, but I cannot force you to do what you do not wish to."

The bear twitched, and the hound thought of all he had lost. The wild man was asking him to go back to that, to care again for it. After two hundred years, it seemed an impossible request. But the wild man was all that was impossible.

The hound began to fear for herself then. She had worried that she would have no role. But the wild man offered no part without pain.

The wild man continued, his voice soft and smooth. "Has the magic done badly for you before this? I think if you look back, you will see it has not. Trust that the magic will teach you the lessons you would wish to know. Trust that if you suffer pain through the magic, it is pain you will look back on and be glad of. Trust that you will be glad to be part of extending the reign of magic from your time long into the future."

The wild man shone brighter and brighter as he spoke, as if he were the sun and there was no need for any other, at least not on this part of the mountain.

Yet the bear held back, a rumble in his throat.

And the hound could feel tiny shivers in her legs that were no reaction to cold.

The wild man put his hands together with a clap. He held them there tightly. His eyes showed concentration. He began to sweat.

The hound could not see what he was doing.

Suddenly the wild man ripped his hands apart, and the hound could feel the sound of it, like an earthquake or a tornado as it tore trees from the ground and tossed them in the wind.

Between the wild man's hands, there was an image of this same place, but at a different time. There was less snow there, and the mountain itself seemed different. The stone shelf was smaller, less distinct, the plants on it higher and more vigorous. Below, the mountains seemed younger.

"There is the past. A time of abundant magic compared to now. A time of less magic than before. A time that is yours as no other time has been."

CHAPTER SIXTEEN

The Bear

"*I* WON'T GO!"

The bear had let his growls rise to a shaking pitch, then found that he was able to make words, though what language they were in he was not sure.

He had not thought of how it was possible for him to understand the hound's language, but now he realized it was the wild man's magic at work. No doubt he could have spoken earlier if he had wished to. Perhaps he should have been grateful to the wild man for this gift, but it seemed only a reminder of all that the wild man had taken from him.

Did the wild man think he could simply send the bear back in time and all would be well? The bear thought of the young king he had been, for only a few years, and how badly he had done. No!

"You say I have a choice. Then I choose this—to stay

here and return to our forest with the hound, both of us untouched by magic," said the bear.

"Untouched by magic?" said the wild man, his eyes boring into the bear's.

But the bear did not flinch away. "By more magic," he added softly.

And the wild man looked away. When he turned back, his face looked ravaged. Suddenly the bear could see hundreds of years of time, of desperation and battling, in that face. Scars, puckered skin around his mouth, sagging black circles around his eyes—this was his own suffering, mirrored back to him and multiplied many times over. For the wild man had lived perhaps since the very beginning of time and magic.

The wild man bowed his head in defeat. "Yes. Yes, you may go. The magic cannot force you back. There would be no purpose in it if you are not a willing warrior for its sake."

How much longer would the wild man live? The bear had never thought to feel sympathy for the wild man, yet there it was. He had fought the unmagic for so long, and yet he knew he could never win for once and all. He could only lose now or lose later.

The wild man sighed. "Once the unmagic has spread too far, there will be nothing left for me to do. No more twists in time, no more transformations of those who will come to hate me for my work, no lonely, cold winters spent with only my own fears for company. Not long at all."

The bear was moved. If he could help—in any way that did not involve taking more magic on himself, and risking the hound with magic—he would do it.

"I would—" he began to offer. Perhaps he and the hound could come visit now and again and alleviate the loneliness. Or they could fight the unmagic here and now, by other means. The wild man had only to tell him how.

Of course, the bear knew, looking at the wild man, that he had already tried all else. This was the last possible hope.

And yet why should the bear be the one to save the magic? What had it ever done for him? He had seen only its worst side. He had never been able to wield it himself. Why should he help magic, and all those who had it, when he would benefit not at all?

Because of the unmagic.

The unmagic had destroyed his home. That was his enemy. Was that not one of the lessons he had learned as a bear? He had nothing to fear from those who wielded magic truly, for the good of humans and animals alike. He had already helped Prince George willingly, in aid of magic. He did not like to think that he simply held a grudge against the wild man for what had been done to him.

He knew what he had been and could see little else that would have made him what he was now.

But he did not want to go back. He realized now that

what he feared was not to be transformed a second time, but to go back to the foolish, shallow boy king he had been.

He did not want the hound to see him that way.

He opened his mouth and touched her shoulder with his paw.

But she would not turn to him.

She pressed her head around his bulk and stared at the gap in time.

The bear looked at the wild man, who wore a surprised expression, though not an unhappy one. "You must know that she will be given a choice as well," the wild man said.

But it was he the wild man wanted, to send back in time as a king! How could the hound—

The wild man said only, "See how the magic calls to her."

Indeed, the hound leaned into the gap in time, her body taut with longing.

"She is a hound," said the bear, though ashamed of himself for saying it. She was not only a hound. He knew that. But it would be easier if she were.

"She is who she is," said the wild man.

The bear gave up speaking to the wild man and spoke instead to the hound. "It is not for you to go there," he said stubbornly.

The hound spoke to him without turning back. "I

will go where I wish. You do not own me. I am not a king's hound, to be bought and sold, or bid to go here and there."

There was such vitriol in her speech that the bear was taken aback.

"I will go," she said again.

"But . . . what place will there be for you there? You are a hound. I will be a man." Had he already moved to accepting that he would go?

The hound said, with a movement to her shoulders that seemed very much like a human shrug, "Then I will be a hound who is a companion to a man. I have been a hound who is a companion to a woman before, and did well enough."

The bear shook his head. "They will not see you as I do. They will think of you as an animal." It was only part of his fear, but it was true enough.

"Let them think whatever they wish. It is not their opinion that matters to me. It is yours. And my own," said the hound.

"You do not know humans as I do," said the bear. "You do not know what they can do, how they can cut with their words, with just a look. You have not felt how it is to be excluded from their laughter or their smiles."

The hound turned from the gap with such a look of scorn on her face that the bear had to step back from her.

"I do not know humans," she echoed. "But it is I who

have lived among humans most recently. Perhaps there are questions you should ask me, about how women take revenge on other women with rumors and lies and cutting words. I think I know humans as well as you."

She knew them too well, and at their worst. Now she would see how much he was like them.

"And think of this," she went on. "If you leave me behind, I will go back to the forest where the unmagic is spreading. I will fight there, on my own, for as long as I can. And when I am finished, I will go in search of the cat man myself, and not turn back until I have killed him. Or he has killed me."

The bear swallowed the bitterness rising in the back of his throat. If he did not wish her to see him as he had been, he would simply have to be better.

"If I go through there, what will I find?" he asked the wild man.

"You will find your own kingdom as it was two hundred years ago. You will enter your kingdom as a man, at the moment that you fled it as a bear. But it is up to you to make yourself king again, for the stories will have already spread about the battle with the animals. The people will know what the wild man has done to you. And they will remember what you have done to them."

The bear touched a paw to the hound. "We will go, then," he said gruffly.

Together they stepped toward the gap.

The magic around it did not bother him as much now.

He seemed to have become used to it. Or he was no longer fighting it.

"One more choice you must make, Hound," said the wild man, stopping her. "He goes as a man, and you may go as his hound—or you may go as a human woman at his side."

The hound let out a short bark in surprise.

The bear wanted to speak, to say that he would never force her to put on a form that was not her own. He had seen how painful it was for her, and he knew how painful it was for himself.

But she was already speaking. "Send me as a woman, for then we will be able to share far more than we do now. And in understanding him, I will be able to help him more."

The bear felt as though he were drowning. She offered him so much of herself, more than he had to give back to her.

The wild man simply said, "Then go through and the magic will do the rest."

He opened his arms wider, and the gap enveloped the bear and the hound before they could change their minds.

The bear howled at the roaring pain in his ears and at the numbness in his paws. He could see nothing. Then he felt the sensation of falling, as if from a great height, but it went on and on.

He came back to himself slowly. He glanced up into the sky, but the wild man's cliff and his moving tree were gone now. He saw only a few clouds and the peak of a mountain that he could sense no magic in.

There was no way back now. The choice had been made, for both of them.

He stretched, and only then did he start at the sight of his arms.

Human arms. Both completely whole and long, but with hair instead of fur and the skin beneath bronze. He stood up on his two feet, and how good it felt to do so! He would gladly walk back to his palace. He tried to think how long it would take.

He had only ever ridden far afield on a horse, and then only two or three days at the most, to observe the edges of his kingdom. On foot and from here in the mountains, it would take at least twice as long, and that was if he pushed himself past all limits.

He turned to look for the hound.

And gasped when he saw her, curled in a ball, gradually coming to herself on the rocks beside him.

She was not the woman she had been before. She did not have Marit's pale, freckled skin and red hair. She was not as tall as a man and painfully thin.

He should have guessed that.

After all, the wild man's magic was not like Dr. Gharn's. It was far more subtle, and far more powerful. And she was not exchanging a body with another creature. She was living in a body that was all her own—only human, and healed of its wounds.

When he thought of it that way, it made sense: the black eyes, the dark, shining hair that fell down her back like sleek skin, and the way she moved, with the grace of a hound.

In addition, she wore a fine gown in a soft red velvet. Her feet were covered in sturdy-looking black boots. She even had a bit of gold around her neck.

Richon looked down at himself then.

He wore the body of the young man he had been, still ungainly and uncertain, but strong. His boots were the ones he had loved once, and the clothes, sweaty and bloodstained, were what he had worn at the end of the battle with the animals. And when he put a hand on the pouch at his side, he could feel the coins that jingled in it.

Had he had coins in his pouch then?

He did not remember. He had not often carried coins with him. He had had servants for such things.

This must be a gift of the wild man.

"Hound," said Richon in his own human voice, not as deep as he had wanted it to be.

He put out a hand.

The hound—the human woman—met it with hers.

"What shall I call you?" he asked.

"Must I have another name, then?" Now she, too, spoke in the language of humans. Her voice was low, more like a man's than a woman's, and not at all smooth. Perhaps it would become smoother as she grew used to it, but the bear did not think she would ever sound like other women.

He would not give her a name. He had imposed on her too much already. But it would be strange indeed if the king referred to the woman at his side as "Hound."

A small smile played across her face. "Call me Chala, for it means 'human woman' in the language of the hounds."

"Chala," he said aloud, trying it out. She seemed to think there was irony in the word, but he thought it fit her well.

CHAPTER SEVENTEEN

Chala

WEARING A HUMAN body again was like having a thorn in her paw. She never entirely forgot about it, but there were also times when she could focus on something else. On moving down from the mountains, for example. A human body was not as well equipped as a hound's, especially not a woman's body wearing a full-length gown. But if she thought only of the next step, and the next, it was better.

And at least she could watch Richon as he also tried to adjust to his new body. It was amusing to see how fragile he seemed. She had been so used to his enormous bear's form, and the thickness of his fur, and the way he could run on all fours or walk upright on his hind legs. Now he seemed all unbalanced, and tottered over rocks that would not have bothered him before. His feet were covered in boots, but still he winced at the rocks underfoot, and he tired so easily that they had to stop frequently to give him rests.

Chala was surprised at the body he had now. His chest was hairless, and so thin and without muscle she could see the line of each rib underneath his tunic. His arms and legs were wiry, but his stomach was soft with food that others had killed and brought to him to eat. Oh, he was handsome enough, she supposed—for a human. His eyes were a clear, bright blue and his nose was unbroken and well shaped. He had broad cheekbones that reminded her a little of the animal that she still saw in him. But was this the kind of man humans chose as a king?

She had seen King Helm and he was nothing like this. Even King Davit, Prince George's father, ill as he was, had had evidence of muscles on his wasted figure. Prince George, too, had the look of a man who did not let others do for him. He was not as good with the sword as King Helm, but he had held his own.

Yet Chala doubted very much that this young man beside her would have lasted more than a few moments in that arena. He might be able to ride a horse well and kill an animal with a spear, but she was not overly impressed with him.

In the world of wild hounds, the male leader of a pack was always the strongest and the biggest. If he fell ill, he was quickly overtaken by another and torn apart. But for humans, it was different. It made no sense, but there it was. The bear had been strong, but it was this weak human who had been king, and was again.

Well, she might be human in body, but she would not go along with that. She would treat Richon as a leader of her pack, and perhaps he would see how to be strong through her.

They spent a full day getting off that first mountain, and then, when dark came, they fell asleep in exhaustion, with no more than a rock as shelter and each other for warmth.

In the morning she stared at her new self in a pool of clear rainwater between two rocks. Her gown was rumpled, the red velvet showing spots of water staining and dirt and one small tear on the hem of the skirt. But that was just clothing. That was not who she was.

She looked closer.

She liked the strength in her lean face, and the long fingernails on the tips of her fingers, like claws. Her hair was shiny black, and fell all over her face in a wild way. Her teeth seemed very white in contrast, and her eyes very black, almost as if she had no irises at all.

She stared longest at her nose, which was long and sharp, as if it could still sniff like a hound's. But it couldn't. She felt the absence of that sense and could only hope it would be compensated for in other ways.

Chala enjoyed flexing her arms, her legs, the muscles in her back and shoulders. She could feel the rush of blood, and it was almost as if she were on the hunt again. So focused was she on herself that she did not speak a word, and it was only when she tried to growl like a hound that Richon stirred.

But he did not wake.

Chala thought how young he was now. He did not even have a full beard, just a bit of stubble. His hair was dark brown, like the bear he had been, and it curled around his ears, damp from the morning dew.

She let him sleep a little while longer, then grew too hungry to keep still. She made enough noise that Richon woke.

"Good morning," he said, rubbing his face.

She nodded to him and then went off to find her breakfast. She found a stream full of fish nearby. She caught a small one, and ate it in one gulp, scales, head, and all. It did not taste as good as it would have to a hound, but it filled her stomach for now and that was all that mattered.

She stopped a moment after she ate and stared out at the birds in the distance, circling the peak where the wild man had been—in the future.

He had not come here yet, though.

Strange thought.

When she came back, Richon was sitting on a rock, one leg tapping out a fast, impatient rhythm.

"I am here," she said.

Richon turned, startled.

"I found fish," said Chala. "In a stream."

His stomach growled, but he did not ask her to show it to him.

"Are you hungry?" she asked. "I did not find any roots or berries. Can you eat any of the grasses here?" She waved a hand at them.

"I suppose," he said, and picked at one strand and put it between his teeth. He chewed it for a while, then spat it out.

"It is not good?"

"I'd rather have a fish," he said.

She stared at him.

"Could you show me the stream? Or . . . I'm sure I could find it myself." He began traipsing in exactly the wrong direction.

Did he have no idea how to find a stream by the smell of it and the sound of the water trickling? Even without her hound's senses, that was not difficult for her. No doubt he was used to a guide of some sort in the forest. But Chala noticed also that he was unwilling to admit that he needed help.

Perhaps that, at least, she could understand from the viewpoint of a hound. One does not show weaknesses to those who might attack.

That he thought she was a danger to him told her only that his life had been one of very little trust indeed. Whoever had been around him, he had had no pack to protect him. And how could one grow strong without a pack?

She caught up with him and tried to steer him gently in the right direction, as a hound might do for a pup.

Richon would have none of it. He seemed angry with her and would not meet her eyes.

What foolishness!

Perhaps a human woman would have let him act stupidly, but that would only waste time for both of them.

She ran ahead of him, then stood directly in his path, her hands tightened firmly around his forearms. It was not until then that she wondered what would happen if it came down to a battle between them, for he was several inches taller than she was, and, lean as he was, still must weigh significantly more.

"The stream and the fish are the other way," she said firmly.

"I will go this way."

"That is the wrong way."

"I will do what I wish," said Richon.

Chala slapped him across the face.

"What?" he said, startled.

"You will not delay us with your stupidity. If you are hungry, I will show you the stream with the fish in it. Then we will be on our way."

He opened his mouth, then closed it. Something crossed his face, a fleeting expression of memory, and understanding. Then he said, "I am acting like a spoiled brat, aren't I?"

She nodded.

"I am sorry. It is this body. I find myself doing what I would have done before, without thinking of it. It is what I was most—" He stopped.

Chala pointed the way.

This time Richon bowed his head and followed her.

She did not get his fish for him, however. Let him do that himself, and grow into the man he should be.

He walked into the stream without taking off his boots, and then proceeded to drench himself trying to grab a fish out of the water. He had no technique, no patience. He would see a fish, leap for it, and find it had slipped away, fully warned by his splashing about.

Finally he seemed to get one, more by chance than anything else. He pulled it out of the water with a wide grin on his face that seemed to transform him from a boy into someone she could see as a king. There was power in that smile.

Did he know it?

He held the fish high, still flopping, and looked at Chala. "No fire to cook it on," he said.

"No time for a fire, either," she said.

He did not argue. He found a stick and pierced the fish through the head to kill it swiftly. Then he grimaced as he dropped the whole thing into his mouth.

It was not a big fish, but it took him two bites to get it down. He struggled with the chewing, then held his stomach afterward, as his face went ashen.

Chala thought it was his conscience bothering him, for

he had sworn to give up eating the flesh of animals as his penance. But surely that was done now! The magic would not keep him living without food here, in this time.

To calm him, she offered: "It is the way of the world. One creature dies to give another life. The fish did the same, killing others to preserve its life. So long as you do not waste."

"I have never eaten a whole fish raw before," Richon admitted, grimacing.

"It is not your guilt, then?" asked Chala.

"I will think of my guilt later," said Richon. "For now, I will try to stay alive."

Which seemed sensible to her. Perhaps more sensible than the bear had ever been.

But it was as if she now knew two different creatures, the bear and the boy king.

She would have done anything for the bear. But for the boy? She felt as if she were starting all over again with him. She told herself that she should feel the same for him, no matter his form. Just as she thought he should feel the same for her, woman or hound.

It was all so confusing.

It had been different before, when she had taken the body of the princess. Then she had never tried to make herself accept the human form. She had known it was not her own. It had only been a disguise.

But this—she had to learn to live with this. All of it.

"You do not think less of me for eating the fish?" asked

Richon, turning back when he found that he had started the journey down the mountain and left her behind.

"No."

"You are sure?"

"You did nothing wrong, of that I am sure. But I will have to get used to you as you are now."

"And I you," said Richon, his eyes taking in her figure in a way that Chala thought was not entirely objective. He had always looked at her with kindness and compassion, but now there was something of possessiveness in his face that she was not sure she liked.

"Your kingdom," said Chala, trying to move his attention away from herself and back where it belonged. "It waits for you. Or do you not care about that anymore?"

Richon flushed. "I care about it. I care about nothing else."

Not entirely the truth, but perhaps as much as he was willing to say aloud. That was the way it was with humans. They did not speak the full truth. They held it back always, so they could appear different than they were.

But Richon the human was also bright and exuberant as she had never seen the bear. It was infectious.

He still could not go long distances without a rest, but he told jokes along the way and laughed at himself more than anything.

Somewhere inside the bear there had always been this human boy, hidden. She could see him try to hide that even now, to put on that older, more sober self. Both sides annoyed her in their own way. But perhaps in time they would come together. That would be a thing to see indeed.

That would be a king who was worthy of the name.

CHAPTER EIGHTEEN
Richon

FOLLOWING STREAMS AND a few trails, they reached the forest at the bottom of the first foothill in three days' time. Each morning Richon woke and followed Chala to get some meat for breakfast. Each morning he ate it raw as she did, and wished that he could show no distaste, as she did. Everything had changed between them.

His old insecurities had returned to haunt him. He was useless as a king, and no better as a man. He could not believe that she felt anything but contempt for him. As a bear, he at least had been self-sufficient. More than that, he had been able to protect the hound against other animals that might have threatened her.

But now he felt as awkward as he had at fourteen, when he had first been made king and realized that he had come to his father's height without his father's wisdom. He had walked for many months with his shoulders rounded, trying to make himself less noticeable, less like his father, as small on the outside as he felt within.

But when his advisers, the lord chamberlain and the royal steward, told him that he looked like a criminal skulking through the palace, he had changed instantly. He had watched the wealthiest, vainest men at his court and copied the way they strutted.

He had felt no better about himself, but no one else had known.

Now he still did not know how to walk as a man. He could walk as a bear, but it was not at all the same.

In some way Richon felt as though the wild man had tricked him.

He had wanted to return to the past, yes. But not as the stupid boy who had pretended arrogance only because he had no other defense.

Two hundred years as a bear, and he had learned nothing that could be used in this other body?

Well, he was not here to make himself feel more like a man. He was here for the magic. And because he wanted to prove that he could be the king his father had meant for him to be, a man who thought of others before himself.

It had been a long time since Richon had allowed himself to think of his father. He had pushed unpleasant thoughts away, telling himself as a king that his father had known nothing, and then as a bear that there was no purpose in raking through the past.

He knew he was not a man of books as his father had been.

Richon remembered that whenever he had gone to his father for advice, the answer had always to be found in a book.

When Richon came to complain about the plain porridge that was served to him at breakfast each morning, his father had held up a finger.

"A moment. Let me think a moment," he said.

Richon waited. And waited.

Then his father leaped to his feet, and ran his fingers from shelf to shelf in the enormous royal library where he spent so much of his time. He climbed atop the ladder, mumbling to himself in words that young Richon could not understand. At last he reached the book he wanted. He opened it lovingly, then blew the dust from the pages.

"My father read this to me when I was—" He looked to Richon. "Yes, perhaps your age. Perhaps younger. I should have read it to you before now."

Then he patted the place at his side on the sedan, and Richon slipped into it.

His father read:

"Once there was a man who ate the best foods at every meal. Sweets and pastries. The richest meats, of every kind. Butters and oils for dipping, and to follow, unwatered wine.

"The man grew fatter each day, but what did he care? He was indulged at every meal and found pleasure in each moment that he ate. If a cook brought him a meal with vegetables or grains in it, he had her sent from the palace. Let her serve the peasants in the streets such fare, but not him.

"Soon the man was out of breath merely from reaching for his food and he demanded that his servants feed him. But they could not feed him fast enough.

"Then one of his servants, a wise old woman, spoke aloud the words that all had been thinking but had not dared to say. She had been his nurse since childhood, and his father's nurse as well. Perhaps it was because she loved him more than the others or perhaps it was because she feared him less.

"'There is no pleasure in wealth if poverty has never been felt,' she said.

"And the man realized that she spoke the truth. He could not appreciate his rich food if he did not have the poor food, as well."

Richon's father held the book open and said, "Well? What is the lesson here?" For there was always a lesson in his books.

Richon creased his forehead and thought. "I must eat porridge so that I will enjoy rich food?" he asked.

His father nodded and closed the book.

Then, at last, he put an arm around Richon. "We love you. We want true happiness for you. That comes with self-discipline."

"Yes, Father," Richon had said. Because there was no other response.

Then King Seltar had let Richon go his way, which was most definitely out of the library.

Now Richon wished dearly that he had spent more time in his father's library. Perhaps if he had he would have saved himself a great deal of sorrow.

But when he became king, the only thing he had seen the library useful for was to sell off its books for money to support his other habits, when the peasants had been taxed beyond their ability to pay more.

All those precious books of his father's were dispersed to other places, perhaps to other kingdoms entirely.

And yet his father's lessons were not the only ones he had ignored. He remembered his mother, Queen Nureen, beautiful on one side of her face but covered with a birth scar on the other. Yet she had never seemed self-conscious about it, had never turned her better side when speaking to others.

His mother had told him once, as she pointed to her scarred side, that it was her obligation to show to others her true face. And her true face had both sides.

"As all people have two sides," she had said.

"Even you, my little one."

Now Richon was startled into wondering if she had had some magical foresight that had shown her that he would become a bear. He had not understood what she meant then. He was only a boy who loved his parents, who loved to be loved and petted and pampered.

But the tantrums—yes, his mother had had to deal with those. That had been the other side to her sunny boy.

Richon could still be embarrassed at the thought of those. Whenever he did not get what he wanted, he had thrown himself to the floor and shouted out threats against anyone in sight: servants, nobles, his own mother and father. He would tell them what he would do to them when he was king.

But his mother would put a finger to her lips and shake her head. And when that did not work, she would turn her back to him. She would motion to all others in the room that they should do the same.

Servants, all.

And no matter what he said or asked for, they would not respond to him until his mother had motioned that they could turn to face him once more. Which only happened when he had finished his screaming, and then his crying, and had turned at last to whispered pleas of forgiveness.

Then his mother would turn around and point to each person whom he had hurt, and he would hang his head and offer apology after apology, then wait humbly until each was accepted.

If only she had lived.

Perhaps she might have made something of him.

But she and his father had died in a carriage accident far from the palace. They had gone out to visit villages at the edges of the kingdom, a tour they took each year so that even those far villagers would feel a sense of belonging to the kingdom, and know that their king and queen thought of them.

He had been told of it by the lord chamberlain and the royal steward, and had never thought to ask them deeper questions about the incident—where his parents had been traveling, who their driver had been, if others had died. He had believed the two advisers his friends then and thought they would tell him all he needed to know.

Now he could see that they had never been his friends. They had told him whatever made him comfortable, even when he deserved no praise. They had never pointed out missteps or shortcomings, as Chala did, that he might better himself.

During the day, he and Chala marched on, sometimes with her in the lead, sometimes with him taking it. But not side by side, and the pace was always so fast that he did not have energy to spare for talking.

What would he talk about, anyway?

Did she want to know how he worried about his

weaknesses? Did she care about the trials that lay ahead for him as king?

No, she expected him to go forward and face whatever came to him with courage and strength—two things that he had always lacked.

Except as a bear.

CHAPTER NINETEEN
Chala

AFTER FIVE DAYS following Richon's fallible sense of direction through forests and fields and over streams, they had at last come in sight of the border of Elolira, the kingdom that would become Kendel, though its borders were not quite the same and there had been many parts of the journey where Chala saw no signs of human civilization at all.

Chala also noticed that animals seemed to give themselves freely to humans here. It unnerved her to see a rabbit pause in its tracks, then turn and look at her, waiting for a moment before it went on its way.

As for Richon, she watched him one morning as he killed his own breakfast. His hand trembled as he stared into the eyes of a partridge, which had gone utterly still as he approached. No hint of ruffled feathers, no attempt to escape.

Do it quickly, thought Chala.

But it was not afraid.

It waited patiently for death at Richon's hands.

He twisted its neck and there was a snapping sound.

Chala let out her breath.

"I hate this," said Richon, nodding to the dead bird in his hand.

"You hate eating?" asked Chala, confused.

"No, I hate it that they die so readily. I do not deserve it."

"You do not deserve to be alive?" asked Chala patiently. She was truly trying to follow his logic.

But he only rolled his eyes. "I don't mean that, either. You know very well that I don't."

Did he think she was playing a game with him? "Then what do you mean?"

"I would rather chase them, I suppose."

"Ah. The thrill of the hunt." That Chala could understand. That was one thing they had in common. Humans and hounds both loved the hunt.

But then Richon confused her again, shaking his head vehemently. "No, I want no thrill from them. But when they give themselves to me, they remind me of my people. So vulnerable, expecting so much, and yet I know I must disappoint them."

"Ah," said Chala. He felt fear, but not as a hound experiences it, in the moment. He felt fear from the past rolling larger into the future.

"I used my own subjects so abominably," Richon said.

"Taxes ever higher, so that I could live in greater style. Laws to make them honor me. Laws to suppress their magic, simply because I had none and did not wish to be shown inferior to the rest."

"But they called for the wild man," said Chala. "So they were not entirely helpless."

"There is that, I suppose," said Richon. He gave her a twisted half smile. "But the animals have no recourse at all."

"You do not know that," said Chala. "If you misused them, they might call for the wild man as well. Or simply stop giving themselves to you. Spread the word among the rest. That is likely why fewer and fewer animals give themselves in Prince George's time. They do not trust the humans to care for the well-being of the whole forest and conserve for the future."

"And that is my fault as well," said Richon grimly. Then he set himself to pluck the bird. He had a hunting knife in the clothing the wild man had returned to him with his form, and he cut off the head. Finally he took the carcass to the stream and washed out the innards.

"I'd prefer to make a fire and cook it," he said when he came back, then waited, as if expecting Chala to tell him no.

She shrugged. "If you wish." She was in favor of anything that made Richon eat more eagerly.

Richon gathered wood, though he seemed to have no idea what wood would burn well and what would not. Chala had watched humans build fires before and remembered which trees were too pungent and which would burn more cleanly, but he must never have paid attention.

Chala did not try to tell him what to do. After all, what better lesson was there than doing it wrong the first time?

She knew that from her own experience as a hound, when she had first attacked a snake and thought it dead. While she had been crouched over it, trying to decide which end to eat first, it had revived enough to rise up and bite her in the face.

She had stomped on it thoroughly afterward, decapitating it with the claws on her hind legs. Only then had she tried to eat it, though the taste was not what she might have wished for, and she could hardly open her mouth by then to chew. She had stayed away from the pack for a few days, until her face looked normal again in a stream, and refused to tell any of the other pups of her encounter with the snake.

She knew at least two other wild hounds that had done the same thing she had and learned the same lesson, for they had stayed away from the pack for nearly the same length of time and come back as quiet and sobered as she had been. None of them made the same mistake again, with a snake or any other kill. And it was her opinion that they became the best fighters in the pack. Later, when she became lead female, she made sure that she always had them flanking her in a fight, for they were the most vicious and the most sure.

Richon would have to learn the same way.

Someone had been protecting him from seeing the consequences of his mistakes. Not a parent, Chala thought. For a parent wishes a child to live long and healthy and to make other children, to continue the line. Those who wish a child to die early because they did not care about the future of the pack might choose otherwise, however.

Chala would have to watch carefully when they returned to Richon's people to discover who it was who had treated Richon in this way. There were advantages in having a hound at his side who looked like a woman. Chala could see that Richon needed her here.

Richon had gathered a pile of sticks and started to build his fire with the smaller ones. He had found a rock to strike against his knife. It took him some twenty minutes until he had a spark large enough to catch his sticks on fire. He had not thought to get anything that would catch fire better than a stick, like bark or cattail.

Even so, the fire smoldered, and he looked up at her, his face alight with triumph.

She smiled back at him.

He built the fire up too fast and nearly smothered it, but took some of the top branches off and blew on it to get it going once more. Then he added fuel more slowly the second time.

Good.

But Chala continued to hold back because he did not wait long enough for coals to form and instead put the partridge on a spit above the flames, so that the skin turned black and the partridge itself fell into the fire when the supporting beams to the spit were burned through.

Richon swore, then leaped into the fire to pull the partridge carcass out. His eyebrows singed, he pulled off one of the legs. It was still raw inside, but he shrugged and ate it anyway. It was only halfway through that he seemed to remember that Chala was there. Sheepishly he offered her the last of the feast.

She shook her head.

"You are angry with me?" asked Richon. "Because I was too eager to feed myself first?"

"No, of course not. Why should I be angry with that?" She thought of the first time the bear had taken her back to the cave and killed a rabbit for her, then refused to eat his share.

There were ways in which she realized she preferred the boy. He had every right to eat what he had caught himself. And no reason to think of her while eating. Another hound certainly would not.

"It was not . . . chivalrous," said Richon.

"You need not use those rules with me. I am not a human woman," said Chala coolly.

"But you are a human woman." Richon nodded to her body. "Or at least the others will think you are. If I do not treat you well, they will take it as license to treat you badly. And they will not think well of me, either."

Chala considered this point. She did not wish to be badly treated, as she had been by the courtiers of King Helm, who had thought his daughter of no value to the kingdom.

So she nodded. "I will take the meat, then," she said reluctantly.

Richon gave her a hunk of it, on a stick that he had crudely fashioned into a fork.

She ate it. It tasted about as she had expected. She grimaced.

"It wasn't very good, was it?" said Richon, after he stamped down the fire and stared at the spit with the remains of the partridge on it.

"I do not like cooked meat in any case," said Chala.

"No, of course you would not. But I thought it would taste like it tasted in the palace. I was looking forward to that. And it did not. Not a bit."

"Which should make you more kind to your cook when next you meet her," said Chala.

"The cook? Oh." He wrinkled his brows. "I do not know if I would recognize her."

"And why is that?"

"I sent my parents' cook away. With a little coin," he added, as if that made up for it. "I did not wish anyone to compare me to my father."

"And the new cook?"

"The lord chamberlain chose her. She cooked well

enough, but I never spoke to her myself. I suppose I should have. But at that time I never thought of giving compliments to those I paid to work for me."

"A hound does not compliment," said Chala. "The task is done for the pack, not for an individual. So all benefit."

"Yes. Well, if only my kingdom truly worked like a pack, I could make that excuse," said Richon. He looked up at the sunlight leaking through the heavy cover of trees.

It was nearly midday already, and they had not begun to move any closer to Elolira.

Chala wondered now if that was part of the reason that Richon had wanted to stop and cook his meal. Had he wanted to delay his approach to his kingdom?

She stared at him and saw the tense line of his mouth, the set firmness of his jaw, and the way that he twitched all over, making the same movement of hand to knee over and over again.

If a hound did this, she would think it had gone mad, and she would have to kill it to protect the pack.

Richon turned an anguished eye to her. "I thought I was ready to return," he said. "I thought I had learned so much. But now that I am back in this body I feel like I am starting over again."

"You will do better a second time," she told him. He was thinking too much of past and future and too little of the present.

"Will I?" asked Richon.

She did not like his mood. She went over to tease him out of it, as she would another hound. She touched him gently on the arm, meaning to call out a challenge to chase her.

Surely a race would return his spirits, and they had never tried it in human form. He would find she had not so much advantage now.

But her hand on his arm made him jump, as if she had touched him with a sword and cut him open.

He pulled back his arm and held it close to his side.

Then he looked at her.

She thought of her mate, so long dead. She did not think of him often now, though in an instant she could recall his scent and the sound of his growl, whether it was playful or angry.

When she had been with child, he had groomed her night after night. It had been pleasant, but she had felt nothing more than that.

He was part of the pack. He had done his duty to her. He had filled the role he should have filled.

And Richon?

He felt like her pack, but in a deeper way. She knew this was not the way any hound would feel. And yet she felt it anyway, part human, part hound.

CHAPTER TWENTY

Richon

I T WAS LATE afternoon of the sixth day when they had found a dirt road at last, albeit one gouged by wagon wheels and split by torrential rain. Chala was ready for a rest and moved to the side of the road. Richon pulled her back.

He put a finger to his lips to quiet her and together they watched as one wolf cub, one wild kitten, one young hawk, and one fawn all lined up in a row behind a line drawn into the dirt of the forest floor.

The hawk gave out a wild cry and the animals all raced forward at the same time, in the same direction. Not one of them attacked another.

They raced to a ring of huge stones, then stopped.

The hawk had won the contest easily, and circled overhead, cawing victory to the skies.

The wolf cub, the wild kitten, and the fawn had all seemed to come across the clearing at the same moment to Richon. He could not tell who had won, if it was indeed a race.

Richon turned to Chala, but she seemed as puzzled by this as he was. Animals might have contests with their own kind, but not outside that sphere.

Then, as Richon watched, the shape of the wolf cub began to waver. The snout shortened. The legs lengthened. And then there was a boy standing in the forest by the other animals.

A human boy, perhaps seven or eight years old.

The other animals also made their transformation back into human shape. The fawn was a young girl, taller than all the others, and with thin shoulders and hips that would make her a fast runner even in her human shape.

The young hawk was the last to change, floating down from his victory flight and turning into a boy of three or four years of age.

"I won! I won!" he chortled.

"You won," said the girl, patting the boy—her younger brother?—on the head.

"He always wins," complained the boy who had been a wild kitten.

"Not always. When we do an obstacle course, he has to swoop back down and up, and then you best him," said the girl.

"Then let's do that kind of race, right now," said the boy.

The girl made a face. "Not now. We're too tired now. And it's my turn to choose next."

"What are you going to choose, then?"

"We've never done a race in the water."

"Water?" asked the boy kitten, shuddering. "I hate water. You know that."

"I know." The girl smiled broadly. "We're none of us really water creatures. That's why it will be fun!"

But the boy was not satisfied. He sulked and said, "Why do I have to be a wild kitten all the time, anyway? Why can't I be a fish sometimes, or a bear, or a bird, like him?"

"If you were a bird," said the girl, "you'd still find a way to complain. Honestly, you take all the fun out of it. We might as well be humans and be done with it." She stood up, brushed herself off, and walked away, her brother following behind, a little jump in his steps as if he thought he could fly.

Richon stared at them.

"They have magic like Frant and Sharla and their children," said Chala.

More magic than Prince George. Magic like that told in the old stories.

Yet Richon had never heard of it before.

"They live here, on the edge of the kingdom," said Richon.

"Yes," said Chala. "To keep safe from your laws."

Richon took in a sharp breath. This was precisely

145

what he had feared, that Chala would see all his mistakes up close and be unable to separate them from who he had become.

"The ones in the past," Chala went on. "Before you met the wild man and learned of the good of magic." She seemed to think it had nothing to do with him now.

Gradually Richon relaxed. "In the future those who are like Frant and Sharla, like these children, will have to live in hiding," he said. "Because of those same laws."

"I do not think that can be all of it," said Chala. "There must be another reason that magic has faded."

"Unmagic," said Richon slowly. He had not seen it so clearly from the future. The unmagic must indeed be part of why so much had changed, so quickly. If the cat man spread it in the forests, it would affect animals and humans alike, and their connection with each other.

That was what he must stop, though he had no idea how one man could do any such thing. Especially a man who had no magic of his own.

Richon's thoughts were interrupted by a whimpering sound in the distance. It sounded like a human child. He beckoned to Chala to follow him, then went back to the edge of the forest and found a small girl with brown hair and clear blue eyes that were filled with tears beside a tree, arms wrapped around her legs.

Richon approached her cautiously, his hands held out to show he meant no harm.

"All is well," he murmured. "All is well."

At the first sound of his voice, the girl startled and froze, her eyes darting back and forth between Richon and Chala. As Richon came closer, she leaped to her feet, clearly terrified.

"I only wish to speak with you," he said. "Please."

The girl stared at him.

Richon half expected her to run away. He knew he did not look his best, in his grimy clothes, with a five-day beard that itched. "My name is Richon," he told her kindly. "And this is Chala."

Chala nodded.

The girl looked away, as if embarrassed.

She could not know him as the king, Richon thought. He was too well disguised and she lived too remotely.

"What is your name?" Richon asked her.

"Halee," she said. Her eyes narrowed. "You haven't any magic, either, do you?" she asked.

"No," said Richon, surprised she guessed the truth so easily. But he was discovering just how little about magic he did understand.

He had always believed magic was unusual and unnatural, something no member of the royal family would ever touch. But here with this girl, hidden in a forest far from other humans, he began to wonder.

He remembered many a time when his father had left the palace without any men to accompany him. No guards, no hunting party. When he came back, Richon had noticed the scent of animals strong on him.

And his mother? She had gone "south to visit relatives" on more than one occasion, and yet she had been
born an only child. When she returned, she had a gleam
in her eye that made him jealous. Why should she enjoy
herself so much without him?

He looked at this girl, the only one without magic
among her friends. How alone she must feel, knowing the
truth about them and about herself.

He had always sensed there was something not quite
good enough about himself. Had his parents lied to him
to spare him that?

"I dream sometimes about what animal I would
change into," the girl said. "I think it would be a fish.
Because I don't belong with them." Her face was pinched
around the lips. "What do you think I would be?" she
asked.

"Oh, you would make a fine fish," said Richon sin-
cerely.

"And you—what would you be if you had magic?"

"A bear," said Richon without hesitation.

The girl looked him up and down again, and giggled.

Richon struggled to look affronted.

"You don't look much like a bear," she said.

Richon rubbed at his beard. He supposed he didn't
look very big or ferocious.

"And her?" Halee asked, pointing to Chala. "She has
magic, doesn't she?"

Richon sighed. "After a fashion," he said. She must

still smell of the wild man's magic, though why it wasn't on him Richon couldn't guess.

"I think she would be a hound," said Halee.

Richon started at this, then said, "Why do you think that?"

The girl shrugged. "It just seems right," she said.

Richon looked at Chala, but he could see very little of the hound remaining in her, and only because he knew her so well. The alertness of her eyes, the way her body moved, the sensitivity of her nose.

"Do you hate them, then, the ones who have magic? Like I do?" she asked.

"Sometimes," he admitted.

"And you're afraid of them, too?"

He nodded. "Or at least I used to be. Now it is not as bad as it was."

"Because you're grown and don't care anymore," said the girl.

"Perhaps," Richon admitted.

"They used to offer to turn me into an animal so I could play with them," the girl said.

"But you wouldn't let them," Richon guessed.

She shook her head. "'Course not. How could I? That's like when you're little and they give you a head start. It's not a real race then." She thought a moment, then bit her lip and added, "I never knew, either, if they could do it. What if they were teasing and I told them I cared?"

Richon could understand that fear.

"I didn't want to play their stupid game, anyway," she said, sticking out her tongue in the general direction of the other children. Then she turned back to Richon. "Only I do, you see? Sometimes I wish I had magic so much I think I might explode." She held her hands tightly together, pressing them against each other until they turned white for lack of blood. She was hurting herself on purpose, Richon thought, to make the other pain go away.

Chala moved closer to the girl and pulled her hands apart, then smoothed them out.

It was the first time Richon had seen her interact with another human. She was gentle, almost like a mother would have been.

There was a voice in the distance calling out a name. "Halee! Halee!"

The girl pulled away from Chala when she heard it. "My brother," she said.

"He has magic?" asked Richon.

She shrugged. "All in my family do. Nearly all in the village as well."

She might have said more, but she was interrupted by a voice from behind them. "There you are, Halee!"

The girl stiffened and it was as if, from Richon's perspective, she had been drained of herself. The pain disappeared from her features, for she would give no sign of it to this brother of hers. But neither could he see her rapt attention and innate intelligence, for she hid that as well. Did none of her family see Halee as she really was?

"Come home now. Mother wants you to help with the washing," said the brother.

"I will come," said Halee. She was holding herself purposely so as to block her brother's view of Richon and Chala.

"Now!" said the brother impatiently. Then he added, "You'll never get your magic unless you learn to obey."

It seemed a cruel thing to Richon to promise the girl something that would never come to her.

Richon watched until Halee and her brother, who had turned into an young eaglet, were out of sight.

Then he turned back to Chala. She took one of his hands, and he felt her warmth spread to him.

CHAPTER TWENTY-ONE
Chala

THEY REACHED A town the next day, on wide, well-maintained roads at last, a full week after they had passed through the wild man's gap in time. Richon said it was called Kirten, and it had a grand marketplace. There were voices calling out everywhere, merchants hawking their wares, people bargaining for the best price, and children running and laughing underfoot.

Chala saw ahead of her a man standing near cages that smelled of animal. When she got closer, she could see that inside one was a small creature with a long tail and a face like a small child's. She had never seen its like before and was intrigued, though the sight of it caged and forlorn made her heart ache.

"Sir, come. Lady, too. See this fine creature. The perfect exotic pet for nobles such as yourselves." The animal trainer held a whip and a rope. He wore a long mustache and no shirt.

"No, thank you," said Richon, backing away, his hands held up.

But Chala, behind him, did not move.

"Ah, the lady has had a long journey, has she not?" He gestured at her dirty gown, which Chala herself had not noticed. She had simply not bothered with it, though she kept her face and hands as clean as she had as a hound.

"Give her something to hold on to, eh? A pet would make her very happy, make her grateful to the man who gives her such pleasure," the animal trainer suggested to Richon with his eyebrows raised and his hands making a rude motion.

Richon tried to pull her away. She knew he was trying to protect her. But she felt a responsibility to protect this animal, and she would not let Richon take that from her.

"What is it called?" she asked the man, trying to buy time.

"It is a monkey," said the man. "And I never give 'em names. Don't want to make 'em answer to something that the new owner will change all over again. What would you want to name it, then? Anything you want, and it will come, I swear to it."

The man was obviously a liar, and not a good one.

"Do you want the monkey?" asked Richon. He did not argue with her, or tell her that this was a whim, as the men she had known as a princess would have done. What a woman wanted was always a whim to them. But

Richon, bear or man, had always done what she asked of him.

She nodded, and he put a hand to his side to get his purse of coins.

But she stopped him with a motion.

"Are there more?" she asked the animal trainer.

"Oh, yes, several. Of course, a lady such as yourself is used to a selection. Come, I will show you the others. There are some variations in color, and perhaps you would prefer an animal that is less—active."

Chala wondered why any human would wish for an animal that had given up its wildness. But then she remembered the many domesticated animals she had seen that had no more of their own language remaining. Cows, goats, dogs, pigs—all had lost half their wildness and half themselves, in her opinion. But at least they had given it up willingly, in exchange for the ease of life with humans.

These monkeys were not the same. They had had no choice in this matter at all, and were given no recompense. She would not have it!

She gripped Richon tightly, and he made a small hiss of pain. Another hound would have nipped her in return, but Richon walked on.

The animal trainer led the way into a stall that stank of animal feces. It was dark and hot inside, and the monkeys in the cages were so weak and without hope that they did not even look up when Richon and Chala

154

walked in. Chala could see old bruises on them and dried blood from wounds that had never been treated, but it was the blank stares that told her how often they had been beaten.

These animals thought there was nothing left in life but that, and they waited for the end. It made her sick to see them.

"This one is young and female," the animal trainer said, pointing to a white-skinned monkey with a crown of white fur on the top of her head.

The monkey did not even look at Chala.

Chala leaned toward it. "Yes, yes, I see," she murmured.

"And this one is a beautiful black male," the animal trainer said, pointing to the one that looked as if it had been beaten worst of all.

"Black, yes," said Chala, pretending interest in something other than the cage and its lock.

The animal trainer seemed to catch no hint of the undertone of anger in her voice. "Perhaps you would like to hold one," he offered.

Chala gave out a long breath, as if she had been holding it for some time. "That would be best, I think. Don't you?" She turned to Richon and let him see the anger in her eyes.

She wanted to kill the animal trainer, to feel his blood in her mouth, to feel his last kicking breath flow out of him.

But that was a hound's desire, and it was not one she could indulge here.

When she had first been forced into the body of the princess, Chala remembered, she had attacked one of the coal boys who had come into her room at night to stoke her fire. She had not been used to being a human and had been angry at the change and at the magic that had been used against her. She had stayed in the castle before, but it had never felt as confining as it did then. Her every breath was a reminder of the prison she was in.

She'd told herself that she would get through this terrible time by thinking of the princess's room as her own den, as she had had in her days with a pack. But the coal boy had violated her territory, had come in without warning, without permission. He had seen her sleeping on the rug near the fire, with the hound at her side, and in his surprise had fallen over her.

The pain had reminded her of other pain, and suddenly it had all come shooting out of her. She leaped on the coal boy and tore into his face with her fingernails, far less effective than claws but enough to draw blood. The coal boy had screamed for help, and it was the princess—in the body of the hound—who had come to his aid. She leaped on the hound and tore her off.

The coal boy ran away and left the castle. Afterward, orders were given for coal to be left outside the princess's room for her to serve herself when she wished it. Slowly the hound had learned to restrain her violent impulses.

It seemed this man had never done the same, though he thought of himself as far above animals.

The trainer got out his keys and whistled tunelessly as he approached one of the cages.

A monkey spit on him as he crossed its path, not out of anger, but because it was ill and wasting away.

The animal trainer threw the cage to the floor and cursed the creature, yanking on its tail.

Chala had had enough. She moved forward, kicked the man's stomach, and snatched the keys out of his hands.

The sound of his howling filled the room, and the animals stared at him, and then at Chala.

She focused on the moment, something easy for a hound to do. She put aside fear and anger, and thought only of what must be done next, so her hands did not shake nor her eyes waver. After trying six keys, she found the right one to open the first cage.

Then she helped the white monkey with the crown of fur out and it scampered away. She moved next to the black-skinned monkey.

Richon stepped between her and the animal trainer.

The animal trainer kicked Richon in the stomach.

Chala heard Richon's gasp, stifled.

It seemed wrong to her that he would have to hide pain even in these circumstances, but she could not spare thoughts for him. She moved to the next cage, opened it, and set the monkey on the ground. But this time the monkey did not move.

"Go, go!" Chala encouraged it in humans words that could have no meaning for the monkey. If only she had some of Prince George's magic, she could speak to the monkey in its own tongue. She had never wished such a human thing for herself before, but she wished it now, for the monkey's sake.

Richon and the animal trainer continued to fight. The animal trainer put his hands around Richon's throat, and Chala heard Richon's choking sounds, his feet and hands scrabbling at the floor.

She went to help, lunging at the animal trainer's back and kicking at the backs of his knees. He turned, surprised.

But the animal trainer's human reluctance to hurt a female doomed him. He did not throw her off fast enough, nor with enough force. And by the time that Chala was on the ground again, Richon was pounding the animal trainer's body and pushing him back, and back again.

Chala took a moment to catch her breath and turned back to the cages. She tried to coax the unmoving monkey to leave once more, but it was no use. A human might have kept at such a fruitless task, but she did not. She could not spend all her time on one animal. There were others who needed her. She felt no guilt. An animal has a right to choose to live or die.

The third monkey that Chala freed wandered away, if not quickly, at least without question. Then she moved down the row of cages.

Richon and the animal trainer fell behind her in a heap.

She told herself that she should let Richon battle alone. No hound would thank her for interference with another hound. But she had to look to him, to make sure that he would survive even if she went on without him.

He was breathing heavily, had a streaming cut above one eye, and would likely have some terrible bruises in the morning, but he was winning. And he was smiling, not at her, but in his own joy at his fight.

Did he know how much that look was like a hound's?

She hurried to the last monkey, picked it out of its cage, then shooed it back toward the forest beyond the town.

Then she waited for Richon to finish.

He seemed to take a long time about it, but she supposed that as a king he had not been taught how to fight.

When the animal trainer lay on his back, eyes closed, blood streaming out of his mouth, Richon brushed himself off and came to her side.

"I think I have never looked less like a king," said Richon, his mouth twisting as he stared down at his clothes.

"And I think you have never looked more like one," said Chala.

Richon's cheeks reddened. "My princess," he said to her, smiling.

Chala knew he meant it as a compliment, but she was not sure if she wanted to be thought of as a princess.

She turned back to look at the man's chest, rising and falling. "Is it wise to leave an enemy alive?" she asked, genuinely wondering if humans had different rules for this than animals. A hound would never leave a threat alive.

"He is one of my people," said Richon. "If I make an enemy of him, whose fault is it, his or mine?"

Chala thought there was a simple answer to that question, but Richon apparently did not agree.

"He lives," he said, with finality in his voice.

They left the animal trainer where he was and moved to other stalls, near the edge of the forest.

Richon stared out into the trees. "Will other animals hurt the monkeys?" he asked Chala. "Out there, I mean. The monkeys are from the south and not used to the animals here. Perhaps we should go after them and make sure they are safe."

Chala was confused. "Go after them and make sure they are safe? You mean cage them again and make them into pets for humans?"

"No, no," said Richon.

"They will die in the forest when it is winter again,"

explained Chala. She had known this when she had unlocked the cages and coaxed them to go. She thought the monkeys must know it, too.

"But then . . . why?" asked Richon.

"Because any animal would rather die free than live in a cage," she said.

Richon breathed out slowly. "And any human," he added.

Chapter Twenty-two

Richon

BEFORE THEY LEFT the market, Richon saw a woman who sat behind a table on which many carvings were displayed. Most of them were mundane likenesses of children or grown men and women, some of animals. One showed a man kneeling beside a hound that he seemed to love, another a girl on a horse, her hair flowing behind her in the wind, an expression of joy on her face.

After Richon had stared at the carvings for some time, the woman looked around, then reached below the table and took out a new set of carvings. These were entirely different from the first. The animals and humans were entwined.

One was a bear's head on a man's body. Another was a woman on her hands and knees with a hound's tail. Another was a hound with a woman's head.

The merchant woman touched a figure of a woman with the claws and eyes of a cat, and the same feral expression on her face.

It was not just any woman, either. There were distinct similarities between the wooden figure and the merchant woman herself.

Richon had no idea why she was revealing herself to him. She might not know that he was the king, but could she not tell, as Halee had, that he had no animal magic? Apparently not.

Last of all, the woman pointed out a figure of a woman connected to a hound, as twins are sometimes connected at birth. The woman did not have a left arm, and the hound was missing limbs entirely on its right side.

Neither could stand alone.

Richon felt guilty at the sight and turned away, thinking of how much of her hound self Chala had already given up.

But Chala leaned forward and touched the figure. "Sometimes two halves are more than one whole," she said.

The woman in the stall nodded. "She understands," she said to Richon. "Perhaps better than you."

Richon pulled Chala a discreet distance away.

"Do you not sometimes wish you were a bear, even now?" she asked him.

"Of course," he said immediately.

"Why?"

"Because a bear can do things a man cannot," said Richon.

"And a woman can do things a hound cannot," said Chala.

"Then you are saying—" Richon began. She could not be saying that she wanted only to be a woman now, could she?

"I am hound and woman," said Chala. "Just as you are bear and man."

"And king," Richon muttered to himself.

"Perhaps the woman there has a triple figure," said Chala. "Shall we ask her?"

Richon was surprised to see the gleam of humor in her eyes. He had seen humor in the hound many times, though it was rarer in the woman Chala.

But her eyes were bright indeed, and when he smiled at her she let her lips spread widely over her teeth.

"Another day we will come back here," Richon suggested. Until this moment, he had not allowed himself to think beyond getting his kingdom back. But now he realized that his kingdom was not enough. He needed Chala, as well, to feel whole.

"Another day?" said Chala blankly. "What need for another day when we have this one?" she asked.

He smiled at her. In a way, he supposed, she was still very much a hound.

And he was glad of it.

164

They had walked nearly to the end of the marketplace when Richon saw a wagon full of books.

His heart began to skip and he hurried closer. He knew those books. They were from his father's library.

The one on the far left was the book on training horses that his father had tried so hard to get him to read. Not that he had offered him bribes for it. His father would never do that. He felt that reading and the knowledge that came from it must be its own reward. He would only show the book to Richon and mention that he had read it when he was a boy, that he had enjoyed it very much.

Then his father might cautiously mention that he had noticed how interested Richon was in horses. He would ask if Richon knew how it was that a young horse was taught to answer to a particular command, or if he knew why a horse should never be allowed to drink its fill after a hard ride.

Richon had been interested in horses as he had been in no other animals. Other animals reminded him of animal magic that he did not have, but when he looked at a horse he thought only of the way it ate up the ground, the feel of air rushing through his hair, and the undeniable excitement of riding up so high.

But to learn about caring for a horse—he thought that was a duty for others.

His father had never forced the matter and Richon had never opened the book. He had not thought about it once in his three years as king. But now he itched for it.

He felt that his horses had deserved more from him, but only now was he able to give it. If he had the book.

Underneath the first one, a little to the left, there was also his father's favorite novel, though King Seltar had not liked to admit that he read such things. In fact, the king had hidden this volume under his own pillow. Richon had found it there and stolen it away, to see if it could be as deliciously sinful as his father seemed to think. He had read more than a hundred pages into it before giving up.

It was only now, looking at the book, that Richon wondered if his father had planted the book under his pillow on purpose to tempt Richon. It had been a young boy's book, of impossible adventures in other lands, and new friends met along the way. But perhaps it was also his father's favorite book from when he was a boy.

Richon saw book after book that he remembered from his father's library. For a moment he felt dizzy, swaying, and imagined the library around him once more as it had been on that last day he had seen it, after his father's death.

His father had labored all his life to collect them in one place, and Richon had cared for nothing but his own feeling of inadequacy at the sight of them.

They were his books no longer.

Richon turned and recognized the man he had sold the books to at the palace. This man had paid in good faith. Richon had no right to demand them back, even as king. He would have to leave them here, and hope that the books went to those who would love them.

But suddenly the man's eyes widened in terror, and he put his hands to his head, falling to the ground in prostration.

"Forgive me, forgive me, Your Majesty," he begged.

Somehow, despite his disguise of filth and a growing beard, the man had recognized the king. And perhaps he remembered that Richon was known for his temper and his whims.

But the man then said, "Do not hurt me with your magic!"

And that surprised Richon.

The man must have heard some garbled version of the story of King Richon being turned into a bear. Otherwise there was no reason for any of his subjects to think that Richon had the least acquaintance with magic.

Richon knelt beside the man. "Stand up," he said.

The man stood slowly, trembling.

"King Richon," he got out at last. "Do you wish to have a particular book back? Or—more than one?" He waved at them. "Take as many as you wish, Your Majesty."

The fear in the man's eyes made Richon see himself again as the selfish, spiteful boy king that his people had always feared.

Well, that must change.

Suddenly the man's name came into Richon's head.

"I want nothing, good Jonner," said Richon. "But thank you for your kind offer."

Jonner stared at him, as if waiting for the truth to come out.

Then Richon had an idea. "If you wish to give me something, there is another thing I would value more than the books."

The man seemed terrified, but he simply nodded. "Whatever the king commands," he said.

"Information," said Richon. "What news have you heard in the last few days?"

"They said—there was a battle. A week ago. Magic," the man stammered out. "And then—you turned yourself into a bear and fled the palace."

Richon looked about for Chala and found that she had drawn herself away from him, watching. He motioned for her to come closer, and felt better when he could smell her breath next to his.

"Anything else?" he asked the man, who looked back and forth between the king and Chala and said nothing.

The man shook his head. Then he bit at his lip and added, "There is something about the southern border."

Richon went rigid. "What about the southern border?" He had always had difficulty with the kingdom in the north, threatening war. But not the south.

"They say that what remained of the army has gone to the border in the south."

"Why?" asked Richon, his head and heart suddenly pounding.

"Because there is another army there, from Nolira, ready to invade. It is said they have been gathering for months now, a new surge with each sign of your weakness, begging Your Majesty's pardon. Now they have begun to attack what little of our army remains after the fight with the magical animals."

Richon felt a terrible weight on his chest. He had known none of this, had never been informed of the gathering army. And had never insisted on being told.

Chala came closer to him and put a hand on his arm, but he could only think of what he had done to his people, to his kingdom.

Jonner spoke again. "Perhaps this is all a ploy. You meant to lure your enemies into battle so that you could defeat them in their pride."

There was a long silence, and then the pressure on his arm from Chala increased until Richon realized he must respond. "Yes," he said. "Yes, of course."

"The money that you have taken to yourself, selling so many of the palace artifacts from your father these last few years—it must all have been spent on secret supplies of weapons and armor. Ah, what a great surprise the king of Nolira has in store for him," Jonner said excitedly.

"Indeed," said Richon, though it was not true. He wished he had been so wise as to plan to protect his kingdom, but he had not.

Why had the wild man sent him here if his kingdom was to be conquered by another? What purpose for a king that was no king?

Well, Richon would not give up easily. And if false hope was all he had to offer, he would not stint of it.

"I will not speak of seeing you unless you wish it," said Jonner. "So as to make sure the surprise is all the greater for the enemies of our kingdom."

"Thank you," said Richon, relieved. He sent the man on his way.

Then he and Chala made their way to the edge of town. It warmed him to see the familiar parts of his kingdom stretching out before him, the waving fields of grain and orchards of ripe, fragrant fruit trees. But he also knew they were several days from the palace.

"We must hurry," said Chala.

"If we are not too late already," said Richon.

Any other woman would have given him reassurance, but Chala gave him the truth.

"If not that," she said.

Chapter Twenty-three

Chala

FOR THE NEXT two days, Richon allowed less and less time for rest. They slept only a few hours at night and hardly stopped for more than a drink from a stream during the day. They ate what they could take from passing fields on the way, and Richon thought nothing of it.

He spoke to Chala only infrequently and with a distant expression on his face. She understood his need for focus. It was animal-like, and she thought it was the right thing to do in the circumstances.

Nonetheless, she was surprised at how painful she found it to spend hour after hour in silence, crossing through a country that was both familiar and unfamiliar at once. She had gone on journeys like this with Marit and had thought the princess spoke far too much, even if it was only a few words here and there.

Now she longed for a few words of companionship. In

the morning she waited for Richon's simple "Good morning" and to be able to speak back to him before his face went blank. She longed to hear his curt "Good night" before they rolled into their clothes and slept near a tree or a large boulder that had been warmed by the spring sun.

She and Richon shared food, and she made sure that she touched his hand when they passed the food between them. She knew that was selfish, but it felt good and she could not resist. She was becoming weak, she thought. Weak and human. Only at night was she a hound, in her dreams.

She thought it must be the magic of this time pressing on her, but the dreams were very strange and vivid. One night she dreamt she left Richon where he lay and went into a forest so thick with trees that there was not even a hint of the stars and moon overhead, and she had to travel by sound and scent.

She wore her hound body again and she could not remember feeling this deeply animal ever in her life. There had been humans everywhere in her world, humans who hunted in the forest, humans close by with their homes and their scents. But here there was no touch of humanity and a peacefulness that held her still.

Then she heard them.

The pack of wild hounds.

There were at least twenty of them, and at first she only meant to listen to them, to keep her distance, and to observe, as she had done once when her daughter was young.

They would not take her presence as a challenge unless she was close enough to be scented, and she knew exactly how far back to stay to avoid that.

But how she enjoyed the conversation among them.

"I saw it first!"

"No, I did!"

"It was my stroke that brought it down."

"But I was the one who tired it."

They argued over a recent kill presumably, but Chala could not smell the blood of it, so the carcass must have been left wherever it had been taken.

"Your greediness was unfair. I deserved more than that."

"If you deserved more, you would have taken it. I am stronger than you, therefore the largest portion of the kill was mine by right. Come and let me show you why, if you wish to argue further."

And then the sound of tussling in the dark, of growling, and nips, of whining when a wound was taken, and then licking and dragging away.

"Any others?"

But it was only a formality. There was only ever one challenge to the lead male of a pack at a time. Unless it was the final attack, and the challenger had already taken charge. Then it would be merely the finishing up of old business, the chance for all of the pack to take a bite of their old leader. As if that would give them some of his strength, some of his memories of the past.

The wild hounds roared out their approval for their leader by howling to the skies, and although Chala could not see him, she knew he would be strutting among them, his head held high, his mate at his side.

She stayed even when the moment was over and the wild hounds were quiet once more, and she hardly heard the flutter of wings overhead announcing the arrival of a full-grown falcon. But when the falcon spoke, she could understand it. It was not the wild man's universal language, but a language of squawks and screeches that she somehow heard as clearly as the language of the hounds.

That astonished her almost as much as what the falcon said.

And then she remembered it was only a dream.

"There is a place of death in the east. Come, all of you. Come and help battle it," the falcon cried out.

Chala's heart grew chill.

The falcon flew away and the wild hounds did not hesitate a moment. They immediately rose up and followed after him.

Chala could hear the falcon continue to give out the same cry as it went along through the forest. And somehow all other animals understood. She smelled squirrels and mice and deer and bears and wolves and wild hounds and all kinds of birds. Frogs and toads and snakes leaped and slithered along. Possums, hedgehogs, porcupines, raccoons, voles, hares, and on and on. There was no fighting among them.

It was astonishing. Animals who came together did so for a battle of survival, and for nothing else. The animals here had set aside their natural tendencies—all of them at once.

It was easy for Chala to go along now that there were so many animals. No one noticed she was not with a pack of wild hounds. They were not focused on the other animals at all, only on the falcon that led them forward.

Chala was surprised again when she realized that she could hear the conversation of any of the animals around her. So it was not only the falcon that was different here. She was changed, too, in this dream. What in reality was reserved for some humans—understanding the speech of animals—became possible in her dream for animals themselves. In some way it felt right to her. It went along with this ancient time and place that had so much magic in it.

"Another place of death so soon? That's twice in a year. It's too much. What is the world coming to?" said one of the beavers, older and with a gruffer voice.

Another spot of unmagic? It seemed even more terrible than it had in the other time, for here the air was thick with magic and life.

Surely it must have a different source. The cat man could not have lived so long, Chala thought. This must be something else entirely.

"We always bring them back to life. With all of us together we have power enough," said one of the younger beavers.

"But if there is more and more of this, there will eventually come a time when we cannot fight it. There will be one dead spot that we cannot fight, and then it will spread like the humans spread, taking far more than is their rightful place."

"That will not happen for many, many years. You worry too much. Think only of the now."

Chala's throat closed up.

Even if this was a dream, those words were true. She knew what it would be like in many years, when the unmagic grew in power. She knew the diminishing sense of wholeness in nature itself.

"There it is!" the falcon called out.

The falcon circled and the animals converged.

Chala was far in the back, but she pushed her way forward and no one tried to stop her. There was no sense of hierarchy here. The animals did not jostle for position, nor give up their place because they knew another was stronger. There was a perfect equality here that Chala had never seen, among animals or humans.

When she reached the front of the line of animals, she saw the cold death at last, and she felt relief. The spot was only as large as her own body, and while it was the same unmagic she had felt in her own forest, it was on a much smaller scale.

Nothing grew around it. She could feel the nothingness that had pulled out all life and brought not even the comfort and familiarity of death. The coldness made her want to whine.

But the animals drew themselves up in a circle around it and Chala felt their magic pulse and stream around them.

Animals with magic.

And she gave magic, too, somehow.

Every moment the spot seemed to grow smaller. It was not so much destroyed as replaced, death with life, but at such a cost!

No wonder the animals in her own time had had no way to combat the unmagic. Or the humans, either.

No wonder the wild man had sent Richon and her back in time.

Chala saw now what had been lost, and it made her want to howl to the skies and never stop. How could the wild man stand it, watching this happen all around him? No wonder he had retreated to his mountain. It must make him ache to see the loss of magic to unmagic as it grew year by year. And he had been watching the change for a thousand years or more.

When the forest's spot of unmagic had been completely replaced with magic, the animals, their work done, began to dissipate.

Chala, too, walked away from the middle of the forest out to where she could see the moon once more. She looked down at herself and realized she was not a hound, after all, at least not anymore. Now she was a human woman.

She had never experienced a dream like this before.

As a hound, she had relived experiences she had had in the past. But this dream was different. It combined bits and pieces of new and old to make completely new stories. Did other humans dream this way?

She woke feeling drained, as if she had bled from a wound. But she did not speak to Richon of it.

Chapter Twenty-four

Richon

AFTER NINE DAYS of traveling, they were nearly at the palace. There was only one more village to go through, and then over the hill and down into the valley. But Richon saw immediately that this village was very different from the towns they had passed through in the north.

The village streets were nearly empty, and those figures they did see were haggard, missing limbs or eyes, starving, ragged, and hopeless. As for the buildings, they were crumbling, roofs unpatched, door hinges broken, with untouched grime everywhere. He saw no animals and very few humans.

Richon wanted to ask someone what had happened, but who to ask? He stared at a man who was walking by, his face down, his shoulders sloped. He moved slowly, as if each step were painful.

Richon reached out a hand to touch him, then let the hand fall.

"Excuse me, sir?" he asked.

The man looked up, blinking. His eyes were red. "Are you mocking me?" he asked.

"No, no," said Richon.

"No sirs here in this town. Not for a long while, and we don't want them coming back, either," he said fiercely.

At this point Richon's clothes looked more like cast-offs taken from a dung heap than anything else. He was glad he did not look like a "sir" much at this point, either.

"Have things gone badly here, then?" Richon gestured at the buildings.

The man snorted. "Badly? That's one way of putting it," he said.

"Will you tell me why?" Richon's mouth felt parched. He swallowed hard and forced himself to continue. "Is it because of the king?"

"King?" The man spat and then stomped on the wet spot that came from his spit. "We don't give him that name around here."

"No, I don't suppose you do," said Richon sympathetically. "Can you tell me what he's done to you, then?"

"Gladly. It's all we ever think about here. That and what we'd do to him if we could put our hands on him," he said.

Richon went rigid at this, but he did not try to escape the punishment of hearing the truth.

180

He only wished that Chala were not there to hear it. She looked away, but he knew she understood all quite clearly.

At least, he told himself, he did not give excuses.

"It was three years ago the king first outlawed magic," the man continued. "Those who were found to use it in the normal acts of living—in planting and protecting crops, in hunting and bringing home to a family meat to eat—they were punished by the loss of a hand on the first offense, and an arm on the second. Here, because it was closest to the palace, the laws were most strictly enforced, in case the king ever happened by."

Richon had signed the laws against animal magic, but he had not written them himself. He was not even sure if he had read them. His advisers, the lord chamberlain and the royal steward, had been eager to help him when he expressed his hatred of the magic. He had not been interested in the details, only in the outcome, which was less talk about magic and less use of it where he could be made to feel inadequate.

Yet he could not blame others for the consequences. He had used his power to take from his people with no thought of their welfare. And if he had read the laws, Richon knew, it would have made no difference. He would have thought the punishments perfectly just. What did he know of townspeople who would lose their livings without a hand or an arm?

"My son was found speaking to an antelope," the man

said. "He was coaxing her toward his knife, for it was close to winter and she was near death. She had no children left to care for. He would have given her a pleasant death and no need to face the cold.

"But the servants of the king caught him with his hand on her neck, and they proclaimed him guilty without a chance of defense.

"They cut off his hand on one side, and then his arm on the other. This, they said, because they were certain he had had more than one offense to his name. Or else how could he have spoken to the antelope so well?

"And then my son found himself without any way to help his family live. He would take no food, though I put it in his mouth myself. He spat it out and said that it was not right for him to take what he could not earn.

"His wounds were not bandaged well. They were not cut cleanly. And soon they began to fester. His eyes went bright with fever, and he no longer spoke the language of humans at all. He raved in the words of all the animals he had ever known, and always he begged for the same thing: his death.

"I tried to keep him close to me, but in the end he broke free. He was still strong then, with the muscles of youth that had not yet wasted away. He ran to the animals he had always loved. I do not know what became of him, but he never returned.

"The king who made these laws killed him as surely

as he signed that law."

I am a murderer, Richon thought. What must Chala think of him now?

But telling the people his identity and allowing himself to be punished would not bring back this man's son. All he could do now was to ensure more men's sons did not die, either because of their magic or because of the war at the border. And he could work to become a king this town deserved.

He stared at Chala and tried to read her expression. He would not try to keep her with him if she wished to go. He could not see what she was feeling. It was so strange, since when she had been a hound she had showed every fleeting emotion clearly on her face. Now that she was human, she hid it all.

But it was the kingdom he would focus on now, and not let himself be distracted by selfish needs.

A young man came down the street as the man finished speaking. The first man waved him over, and said, "He wants to hear your story, too, no doubt. Tell him about your father. What the king's laws did to him."

The young man looked at Richon, eyebrows raised, as if to be sure Richon wanted to hear it, after all.

Richon nodded. Hearing it was the least he could do.

"Please tell me," he said.

And the young man did.

"My father survived the first year of the new laws

without being caught. He learned to be cautious. He only showed his magic when there were no strangers about in the village. He did not use it beyond the borders of the village, either, because there were too often soldiers there, protecting the king's own animals for his hunt. All animals belonged to the king, it seemed. As all people belonged to him. And all magic.

"But then the rewards were announced. A dozen gold coins for each man who was betrayed to the king's men. They came through each year. The first year no one in the village betrayed another. But the second year it had been a bad harvest. Too many of us had been afraid of the king's law against magic. We had not asked the beetles and worms to irrigate the ground for us. We had not called to the birds to keep from our fields.

"And so we were starving, all of us, when the news of the rewards came. My father, as well as many others, was betrayed that year. Those who betrayed them were equally betrayed, for they received no payment at all in return for their loss of honor.

"When the day of the executions came, they were forced to speak their accusations aloud before all in the village, and to watch as the sentence was carried out against those to whom they had meant no harm.

"We all watched as they died, and perhaps the king expected that there would be yet more deaths, that we would turn against those in our village who had turned against us. But we saw the true enemy, and it was not those who had spoken out in their need. It was the king."

Richon clenched his fists and told himself he was not yet done. There was more pain here for him to share.

Finally a girl came, no more than eight years old. She spoke with a lisp, and her voice was so childlike that Richon was chilled to hear it speak with such anger. She said:

"My mother had no magic. My father left us long ago, and it was his magic I inherited. I used it in fits and spurts because I had no one to teach me. My mother tried to tell me that it was wrong, but it was as if she told me to stop eating a sweet. I held it in my hands—how could I let it be wasted?"

She ought to have all the sweets she wished for, Richon thought. Now, when it was too late for her to be the child she should have been.

"She died because of the magic I used," the girl said. "I made a locust dance on my hand. A man saw me and sent to the king for his reward. When the king's men came, my mother insisted that it was her magic that had made the locust dance.

"And so she died in my place. Her last words to me were that she loved me and to remember that I was only a child. But at that moment I grew up. There are no children when a king like that rules over us."

Richon suspected there were many more stories, just as bad.

In time, if all went well, he would invite these villagers to the palace to tell him the rest. And he would make what compensation he could to those who remained.

CHAPTER TWENTY-FIVE

Chala

C HALA AND RICHON reached the palace on the tenth day after they stepped through the gap in time. The dust-colored stone towers were plainly visible against the acres of cleared land. There was no moat, but the gates were twice as tall as any human, with pointed spears on top to prevent incursions. There was a tower on either side of the gates, but the lookouts that should have been filled with guards were empty.

There was no one to be seen, however.

And when Richon pushed against the gates, they creaked open.

Was it possible that Richon had been king here only days ago? It looked as if the palace had been abandoned for months.

Why should humans wait to make a new leader when a pack of wild hounds would not?

"Perhaps you should wait here," said Richon.

Chala growled low in her throat and did nothing of the sort.

Richon walked carefully on the overgrown stones and then through the gates. Chala followed behind, conscious for the first time of how little she looked like the companion to a king. Her hair was matted with sweat. Her skin was scratched and dirty. Her gown looked more gray than red.

Yet she kept her head high and walked onward.

The cobblestone path led to a courtyard faced on three sides by the palace itself. Inside the courtyard, Chala began to walk more easily, her breath steady in her throat, her feet light. Somehow the stained-glass windows and cut stone around them made Chala feel almost as if she were back in the forest, giving her a sense of peace and tranquillity.

When Chala looked more carefully, she could see that there were abstract figures of animals embedded in the center of each window. One had a deer, another a wolf, a third a bear.

Had Richon ever noticed them before? Had he seen how the palace was homage to the animals of the forest, and an attempt to re-create it here in a human way? Chala had never spoken to Richon about his ancestors, but this seemed to her clear evidence of the animal magic in those who had built the palace. There was love of animals and knowledge of their way of life in every stone here.

Richon walked more and more slowly through the courtyard, and then he ducked his head under an arch. Under the light was a garden, or the remains of one.

"This was my mother's place," said Richon. "My father cut it out for her and she came here nearly every day. Sometimes she brought me with her, and I sat and watched her dig in the dirt with her hands—she would not wear gloves.

"After she died, I kept this. So many reminders of my parents I destroyed or sold, but this I could not touch. I did not come to see it, but the cook made sure that the herbs were cared for, and she watered the bushes."

His shoulders shook and tears streamed down his face; he knelt on the ground, his hands touching the dirt, his nose turned to the dead bushes.

When humans wept, what did other humans do? In King Helm's court Chala had seen them laugh or make snide remarks. Or, if the cause of the weeping was an attack by another, it seemed to invite a second attack, or a third. Especially among women of the court.

Only once had Chala seen a man touch the shoulder of another man gently. But the weeping man had thrown the other off with a vehemence that Chala had been surprised to see in any human. The rejected man's jaw had grown taut, and his eyes glassy, staring nowhere at all. Then he had moved away from the weeping man.

A wild hound snarled or bit when in pain. A wild hound used claws as weapons, sometimes on its own flesh. But once a hound began to whimper in pain, it was either near death or wild no longer.

She had never been uncertain before. She hated the feeling of it, like a loose cloak over her skin that rubbed against her neck with every step.

At last Richon got to his feet and walked, head bowed, away from the small garden. He began to move through the palace itself, room by room. The kitchen smelled of dusty spices and was full of broken tools. In the servants' quarters Richon seemed unsure of himself, and he turned back and back again before returning to the courtyard.

"My own palace, and I don't know its secrets," he muttered. He led her through the main hall and through the larger, obviously royal rooms. The fine tapestries had been taken from the walls and left pale shapes behind, marking where they had been. Finally Richon stopped at a door, his hand to his heart.

"It has been so long," he said. Some part of him seemed to grow smaller as he walked through.

It was a large room, empty but for a child-sized chair that had been smashed and lay on its side. Richon bent over the chair and ran a hand smoothly over it.

For a long moment he stared into the cold, empty fireplace.

Chala wanted to shout at him, to demand he tell her what he felt. As a hound she had been able to read emotions in other hounds just by the way they stood. Even with the bear she had been able to see what he felt in his stance, and smell it in his breath. But with this man she was at a loss.

At last Richon said, "The royal steward and the lord chamberlain came here to tell me my parents were dead. I did not believe them at first. I kicked and screamed. And when I was finished at last, they told me that it was time for me to give up my childish habits, for I was to be king.

"After that day I never came back to this room. I was trying so hard to be a grown man that I dared not remember how much I had loved being a child. I do not even know what they did with the playthings I had here—if they waited for me all those years or if they were taken away from the first."

He paused for a long moment and then sighed.

"I should like to have had one to give to a child of my own."

Chala stiffened.

She thought of him married, sharing this palace with another woman, giving her his child. She could not think of a human woman she thought would deserve Richon. A human woman would surely drill the wildness out of him.

Yet the most she could hope for was to stay and watch, hoping that Richon did not send her back to the forest to live without him. He knew all too well that she might look like a human, but she was a hound.

Richon moved on, and Chala matched his strides

without thinking. They passed through the throne room, which was empty and stank of urine—and worse. Someone had taken the trouble to truly foul the place before leaving.

Then the ballroom and the dining hall. Richon looked each of them over, surveying the damage stonily.

Then they went to the stables.

Richon walked by each stall.

He stopped for a few seconds longer at one that had the name Crown burned into the door.

And then, near the far end of the stable, there was a noise.

"Who's there?" called Richon.

The reply came in a snort and a whinny.

Richon's mouth twitched into a smile. "Crown?" he said.

The whinny came again, and this time Chala could hear a note of desperation.

"Crown, I'm coming," said Richon. He moved cautiously through the other end of the stable, looking in each stall.

He found Crown lying down, one eye nearly shut with crusted pus. One leg was broken, and there was a terrible slash that must have been done deliberately with a sword down his belly. That he had not been killed was a miracle, but not a kind one.

He should be put down, thought Chala. No animal would wish to live through this. Nor any human, either.

But she did not know if Richon had the strength to do it, not after what he had been through this day.

Richon helped Crown to stand on three legs, and the horse seemed happy, but only for a moment.

As soon as it was standing, Richon had a look at the bleeding sores on the horse's side. Its body, which must once have been the pride of the king's stables, was now withered. It was clear that the horse had gone without water for far too long. It would die within the day, in terrible misery.

Richon put his head close to Crown's. There were no more tears flowing down his face, as there had been in the garden. He did not look devastated as he had in the child's bedchamber. He looked determined. And Chala knew then that he could bear the horse's pain no better than she could.

He went back through the stalls, his voice calling back to gentle the horse in his absence.

While he was gone, Chala moved closer to the animal. He was too far gone to care if she was a familiar hound or not.

She only meant to comfort the horse while Richon was gone. She put a hand out to touch the horse's belly, near the infected sword wound. And with that one touch, she suddenly felt all of the horse's pain and deprivation. It was as strong to her as if she were close to dying herself.

She pulled back, trembling.

What had happened?

She had become the horse, in a way. But that was only possible through magic.

Impossible.

And yet she had had magic in the dream. If it was a dream.

Chala put out her hand once more. The pain of the horse flowed into her, and then she let her strength flow out.

Chala did not remember anything of herself for a long time after that.

But she remembered what the horse remembered. She saw the man standing above her, the one called Lord Kaylar, holding the sword, the vicious look in his eyes, her horse legs tied to posts so she could not turn away. She remembered the sound of terror that had come from her horse's mouth and then the man's laughter, mocking her agony.

And then, in and out of pain, in sleep and waking, the fever that had come and then finally passed, leaving her weak and trembling, waiting for death.

And the king, at last, who came to help her.

Chala felt it all through Crown.

And when she woke, Richon was standing over her, holding a short, rusty knife.

Dropping the knife, he fell to her side. "What happened?" he asked, his eyes dark with concern.

Chala lifted her head—a human head again now—so she could see the horse. It was nearly healed. There was

194

a scar on its belly, but the sores on its side were gone and it stood on all four legs now, no sign of a break on any of them.

"Magic," said Richon, staring at her with awe on his face. And not a little pain.

Chala understood immediately, for in seeing Crown healed by her, Richon was faced once again with the fact that he did not have the magic. He had not been the one to heal the horse he cared for.

There was a long silence, and then Richon offered her his arm. They walked out of the stables together, Crown behind them.

Chala stared at the horse and thought of how much faster Richon could go if he rode it, alone, to the border where the army waited.

But Richon patted his horse and said, "You've served long enough here. It's time for you to be free of this palace and all that has happened to you here."

Letting Crown go was the kind thing to do for the horse. And now Richon could hold to his memories of how the horse had once been with him.

In the silence that followed, Chala and Richon turned and walked to the south side of the palace. He did not look back, only forward—to the battle that lay days ahead. And this time Chala knew her purpose. She had magic after all, and she would use it to defeat Richon's enemies.

CHAPTER TWENTY-SIX

Richon

FOR THE NEXT two days, Richon and Chala traveled together silently. Richon felt that seeing the palace empty had cleansed him in some way from the ghosts of the past. He did not understand how Chala had healed Crown or how she had found a magic that he had thought was always reserved for a select group of humans, but his pain faded when he decided that it must be a gift from the wild man, like the coins he had found in his purse. To be used when necessary, but once used, gone.

They soon came to another village, not as devastated as was the last one, and Richon sighed with relief at the sight of the women and children working in the fields, and in the shops along the market streets. Chala watched them intently.

There was a bakery with heavy dark bread for sale. Richon bought one loaf and paid for it with a copper piece, but Chala insisted on buying two more loaves and paying a full silver for hers, though that was three times the price posted.

The woman who worked the shop stared at the coins, as if afraid, until Chala said, "For your children's sake."

The woman nodded but said nothing. Her eyes watched Chala suspiciously until she and Richon left the shop.

"Why did you give her so much?" asked Richon.

She waved an arm. "All of the men in town are gone. Only the women and children remain."

"Oh," said Richon, ashamed he had not noticed. His mind had not been trained to think of details like this about his own people. He had always thought of them as a group, not as having lives of their own.

Chala was better able to understand his people than he was!

They passed a blacksmith shop, and then Richon turned back as he realized there was a man inside. The only full-grown man in the village.

The blacksmith was hard at work pounding out a sword. But when the blacksmith turned to him, Richon saw the man was missing an arm.

"I haven't finished yet," the blacksmith said roughly.

"Finished what?" asked Richon.

The blacksmith paused a moment. "You are not a messenger from the royal steward?" he asked.

Richon shook his head. The royal steward? His mind

whirled. Was that who was in charge of his armies at the border?

Once Richon had thought the royal steward his loyal adviser, but in his years as a bear he had realized that the man had simply been interested in taking power for himself through a weak king.

"Ah, well. I have no time to spare to make orders for anyone else," said the blacksmith. "The royal steward has paid for all the weapons I can make for the next month, and more than that besides. So even if you've broken a plow or have a horse in need of shoeing, I cannot help you."

His eyes glanced over Chala, but he said nothing of her. Too much work made a man incurious, Richon thought.

"I see." Richon thought to leave the shop then, but stopped to ask one more question. "The men of the village?" asked Richon. "Did they all join the army to go with the royal steward?"

"Join the army? I suppose you could put it like that," said the blacksmith with a trace of bitterness.

Richon noticed how awkwardly he worked with his one arm. The flap of skin that covered his stump was not entirely healed. How recently had he been maimed? And how had it happened?

"How would you put it?" asked Richon.

"Forced to it," said the blacksmith. "Threatened with the lives of their wives and children."

Chala made a very human sound of distress as the blacksmith went on.

"Took some of them hostage, sent away to other villages. No one knows where. Most of them were left here, though. With the royal steward's promise the men would be home by winter."

Did the royal steward think the war would be over so quickly?

"And you?" asked Richon.

The man held up his stump. "I resisted," he said. "The royal steward took the sword right from my own shop and cut off my arm with it. Said I was lucky, for he needed blacksmiths at home as much as he needed soldiers. Said I would live so long as I proved that I was useful. And he told me the number of swords I was to produce each month." He named a figure that made Richon's eyebrows rise.

"Indeed. I work night and day, and still I do not meet his quotas."

"And what will happen to you if you do not?" asked Richon.

The blacksmith held up his other arm.

Richon swallowed.

He remembered the royal steward's cruel sense of humor. It was no stretch to believe that he would do what he had said to the blacksmith and laugh over it. But it sickened Richon to realize that he himself had laughed with the royal steward for so many years, and in no better causes.

199

"I will take those swords to the royal steward if you like," said Richon. "I am going to find the army myself, to join with them."

"Why?" The blacksmith was surprised and looked more closely at him. "You look familiar."

Richon stiffened, but could not think how a blacksmith would have met the king.

"Well, no matter," said the man flatly. "If you're going to the battlefield, I won't be seeing you again. One way or another you'll be dead, and the rest of us will be taken by Nolira."

"Doesn't it matter to you if our kingdom is taken by another?" Richon asked.

The blacksmith shrugged. "One king or another—they take our taxes just the same."

"Is that the way you truly thought of your king?" Richon asked.

The blacksmith thought a long moment. "I suppose—I felt sorry for him," he said at last.

"Sorry? Why?" This was the last thing he had expected. Anger or jealousy, yes. But pity?

"He did not see how little he ruled the kingdom, I think. He believed he made the laws and the people listened to him. Perhaps those who lived in more far-reaching places believed that, too. But those of us who were near enough the palace—we saw the truth. He was a boy being pulled by a nose ring, like a pig to the slaughter. And he had not the least idea of it."

"He should have known it. He should have been stronger," said Richon darkly. "That was his duty, as king."

The blacksmith sighed. "Yes. We all have our duties and we all fail in them at one time or another. Some fail more than others, I suppose." He held up his one hand. "And some are given more obstacles to overcome. But I do not blame him. He was used as much as any of us were."

Richon walked away from the blacksmith's shop with a heavy burlap sack containing five well-crafted though hastily made and undecorated swords, all wrapped together. He carried them on his shoulder, and in his mind he carried the blacksmith's evaluation of himself.

It was like being told that all his mistakes were, in fact, a great deal smaller than he had thought they were. Because no one had expected more of him.

After a long moment, he felt Chala's hand on his shoulder. It was light but warm, and he looked up at her in surprise.

"I do not know what to do," she said. "You are a human. You deserve to have a human response, but I do not know what it should be. If you would tell me, then I would do what would comfort you. If that is what you would like."

It was a strange speech, but Richon could see it was entirely serious.

"It is not my place to tell you what you should do," he said. "Not even a king can order another to give him comfort. If it is commanded, there is no true power in it."

"But what if it is offered the wrong way, or if it goes on too long, or if there are others watching—" Chala stumbled over the words.

"It is your choice," said Richon. "You must do what you wish to do."

"And if it is not what you would wish?" asked Chala.

Richon wanted to sigh. "I will always appreciate your touch, Chala," said Richon.

Her eyes widened. "Are you sure?"

He nodded. "I am sure."

"Oh. That is not so difficult, then."

Richon used her hand to pull her closer to him so that her face was only inches from his. He could smell her breath, and thought how it had smelled when she had been a hound and he was a bear.

"Do not be afraid of me," Richon said. That she thought she needed to be more for him! When he could see so clearly that it was he who needed to be more for her. For all of them.

"I may do the wrong thing. I may embarrass you among your own people," said Chala.

"Never," said Richon fiercely.

"I am a hound," she said.

It was not an apology, simply a statement of fact. And

for Richon to deny it would only make Chala think him a liar.

"You are a hound," Richon agreed. "But you are more than that."

"Am I?"

"You are."

"I am not human. I will never be—fully human," said Chala.

Richon swallowed and thought of Chala paying her silver for two loaves of bread they did not need. "You say that, and yet there are times when I think you are more human than I."

Chala tilted her head to one side, as a hound might who was listening for a distant sound in the forest. But she did not argue with him.

He let her hand go, then they walked away from the village together. Once, later that day, as they moved into the southern hills, he thought again of the village children waiting for fathers to come home. He felt Chala's hand on his stiff back muscles, rubbing at them ineptly but with kindness.

Long past dark, when he was drenched in sweat and so exhausted that he was stepping over Chala's feet, as well as his own, he stopped at last and let himself rest.

He did not think he would sleep, but he did. He woke in the middle of the night, breathing hard from a dream in which he had seen soldiers dressed in his own colors being slaughtered by the hundreds. Chala woke with him, and put a hand on his arm.

He pulled himself closer to her, then let her go with a curse at himself.

He had said he believed she was human in many ways, but he still did not know what name to give his feelings for her, and it seemed wrong to offer less than his whole self.

He did not sleep again, but he woke Chala at dawn with a rough shake to her shoulder.

Partly because he could no longer stand his own stench and partly because he wanted to punish himself, he took a very cold bath in a stream nearby. Chala waited until he was finished scrubbing himself and his clothes and had gotten out to shiver in the dying sunlight before she did the same.

In the following week they passed more villages and heard more stories of the royal steward.

He had insisted that ten women from one village be sent to the army at night, to offer "companionship" to the soldiers. The women who remained to tell the story would not meet Richon's eyes.

Another village told of the royal steward's demand that all their sheep be slaughtered and sent to the army for a night of feasting. Ten of the men from the village had agreed to join the army then, for there was nothing left for them at home, now that their flocks were gone.

Richon could even imagine the royal steward explaining that it was all for the best, that the villagers would be grateful for their part in the great victory of the kingdom, and would be able to tell tales to the next generation of bravery and fighting at the side of the royal steward himself.

Richon thought of the wild man and wondered if he had even begun to discover what it was the wild man had sent him here to do. He wanted desperately to save his kingdom, but the wild man had been concerned about the unmagic and Richon had seen nothing of that.

Chapter Twenty-seven
Chala

FOUR DAYS AFTER leaving the palace, they were between two villages, on the edge of a forest, when Chala caught sight of a cage as large as a man standing upright on the ground. It was shaking and she could hear animal sounds coming from it. She thought immediately of the monkeys she had freed before.

Why did humans think they should be allowed to do such things to the animals they shared the world with? It was one thing to kill animals because of the need for food, and another entirely to imprison them like this.

Richon tried to hold her back. "You do not know what danger there may be in that cage," he said.

But she shook him off and ran toward it. She recognized the language of the wolves, which was very close to her own language of the hounds, and she called out, "Be calm! I come!"

But it only made the creature in the cage more agitated. The cage swayed from side to side and then turned over. Instead of angry words of demand, Chala now heard calls for vengeance, for death, for blood against all humans.

She looked back at Richon, who could not understand the words at all, but must have gathered the general meaning from the tone in which they had been spoken. He did not look pleased, but neither did he suggest that they ignore the noises and simply walk past the cage.

He had been an animal recently himself, treated by humans as nothing more than meat to hunt for.

"I must do something for it," Chala said to Richon.

He bit his lower lip, but then nodded.

Chala approached the shaking cage.

She kept thinking of the animal held inside as a "creature" rather than as a wolf, although it spoke the language of the wolves quite clearly. Why was that? Because the animal's voice did not sound like a wolf. It was too high-pitched.

She knelt down. The cage was filthy and it stank, and she wrinkled her nose and nearly turned away from the terrible smell.

But then she saw the creature's eyes, and they were blue.

A human blue.

She leaned into the cage. There was little hair on the

creature except on its head, and the arms were long, with rough fingers. No claws, either. He stood on all fours like a wolf, and he was matted and filthy so that his color looked dark.

But it was a human boy, perhaps fourteen years of age, in the middle of that time between childhood and adulthood.

He showed his teeth to Chala and then tore at her face, which she had placed too close to the bars.

She drew back.

He growled and called out in the language of the wolves, "Mine—this one is mine."

It was the traditional call at first sight of prey, and it meant that the other wolves, while they could help to corner the fleeing animal and would certainly share in the meat, would also give this wolf the opportunity to make the first killing strike against it.

Then all would converge and the pack would feed.

Richon came running up and put an arm around her. He turned her so that she was facing him. "Are you hurt?" he asked.

She shook her head.

"What happened?"

She pointed to the boy.

"It's—" said Richon, then he paused. "Impossible," he muttered.

But it was possible, obviously, since the boy was here.

"There is something gravely wrong here," said Chala. How had this boy been made so animal-like, and who had placed him in this cage?

She turned to Richon, and he moved a little closer.

"Do you have a name?" Richon asked, pronouncing each word distinctly. He kept his hands and face away from the cage and stared intently at the boy.

There was no sign of understanding, as far as Chala could tell. Was it possible the boy had never learned the language of humans?

"The story of the boy raised by wolves," said Richon, glancing at her.

Chala nodded. She remembered it as well. But the story had not spoken of how difficult it might have been for the boy to return to humans.

"You think he was raised by wolves but that humans tried to take him home and found he was too much animal?" She thought of herself and how much she was like this boy.

"It is all I can think of," said Richon. "Perhaps he lived too long with the wolves to ever make the change." He did not look at her. "In any case, they should have sent him back to the forest with the wolves once they discovered that he could not live as a human."

"Unless they feared he could not survive," said Chala.

She looked around now and saw evidence of bones that had been eaten clean and thrown outside the cage.

209

The boy was being fed at intervals and brought water as well.

She could not tell how long he had been in the cage, but he would survive here. Animals from the forest could not hurt him, no matter how they might be attracted by his calls. In that sense the cage was for his protection. But it also kept him in one place so that the humans knew where he was and could come to him to keep him alive. The humans cared for him, though their way of expressing it might seem strange to Chala.

"He is also one of my subjects," said Richon bitterly. "And I have failed him."

"What do you think you should have done to help him, then?" asked Chala.

Richon thought for a long moment. Then he said, "If I had magic of my own, then I could tame him. Or if you had not already healed Crown with the magic the wild man gave you, perhaps you could do it."

Chala stared.

He thought that she had healed Crown with magic from the wild man?

She did not have time to explain now. She had to help this boy with her magic if she could.

Before Richon could stop her, she reached the cage and put her hand through the bars, reaching for the boy.

He leaped toward her. She felt his teeth dig into the flesh of her arm.

"Chala, no!" shouted Richon.

But she was already gone, into the magic, and was far from him.

She went into herself first, feeling the thread of magic that connected her to the boy, pulling herself along it as if she were on a rope bridge crossing from one side of a river to another.

She could feel that he was sucking at her blood, and might do worse, but there was no pain as yet.

With her magic she could see his life growing up with wolves. Then the day that he had been discovered by humans, who had gone into the forest to seek for the source of the magic they felt from far away. They took him away in chains and they tried to teach him, to no avail. And so had come the cage, and their infrequent visits.

How he hated them!

How he hated everyone, even himself.

But only because of his human form.

His soul was a wolf's.

Chala saw clearly that to be saved he must be allowed to become a wolf in truth.

She could only assume that the animals in the forest did not know how to use their magic for something like this, or that they did not have enough of it. Perhaps she did not have enough, either. But she had to try.

She pushed her magic toward him.

She did not know precisely what she was doing, but she had been next to Prince George as he had changed her back into her hound form, and the princess to her woman's form.

Hairless skin turned to fur.

Ears peaked.

Nose turned to snout.

Teeth and limbs elongated.

And then it was done.

The boy was a wolf.

Chala fell back, breathing hard, blood streaming down her arm.

The wolf growled at her, still not sure of what she had done. But he did not seem as crazed as he had before. He was himself again, though with less magic now to draw humans to him. He only needed to be set free, and allowed to return to his pack.

Chala pulled on the lock to the cage but could not get it to come free. The use of magic was so unfamiliar to her.

At last Richon, hands trembling, came around her and put his knife in the keyhole. It sprung free and the wolf leaped out.

Chala watched him go, and felt a terrible wave of envy. He could return to the forest and be at home once more. He could be a wolf again, with a pack and a wolf's life.

But with all her magic she did not know if she would ever be a hound again. She did not regret the choice she had made to be a human woman and take on the task of aiding Richon against the unmagic.

It was the simplicity of life as a hound that she missed. The physicality of it. Eating, the sun on her bare back, even the feel of rocks in her paws. And the sense of belonging, in the forest with other animals, of her kind and not.

She did not know if she would ever truly fit in with humans. She did not know if she wanted to.

"Chala," said Richon.

She felt him close to her, his touch easing the sting of the wound on her arm. He tucked her head into the crook of his neck, and she knew that here, at least, she belonged. With him.

With surprise, she noticed there was something rolling down her face, stinging it. She put a hand up to feel it and discovered her face was wet.

Tears.

She was weeping, as a human woman would.

"I thought it was the wild man's magic that you used with Crown," said Richon after the tears had stopped and she had pulled away from him once more.

"No," said Chala softly.

"You have it because you are human now?"

"I think it is because of this time and place. There is magic everywhere here and in adundance. Even the animals have it."

Richon slapped his leg and swore darkly. "I am surrounded by magic and have not a drop of it myself, though I am supposed to be king. Truly I think I fit better in Prince George's time than in my own."

Chapter Twenty-eight

Richon

RICHON'S HEAD ACHED with the weight of his weaknesses. He desperately wanted oblivion, and he wanted to be alone. He was not proud of himself for it, but drink had always given him both of those things in quantity.

At the next town that looked as if it were large enough to have an alehouse, he put down the sack of swords and told Chala he planned to go in. He half expected her to chide him. He had been so insistent they needed to hurry toward the army.

But she simply nodded and said that she would wait and look after the swords. She also made a face that reminded him of the time when, as bear and hound, they had come across some rotting grapes. His nose had been pricked by the reminder of the scent of wine, and he had licked at the grapes. She had turned her nose up, saying she knew where better food was to be found.

All he wanted was to not think about his own lack of magic for an hour or two. He went inside the alehouse.

The two men inside stared at him. One wore a patch over one eye and had a beard that looked as though it might be crawling with lice. The other was so drunk that he could hardly hold his head straight.

"Good morning," Richon said after a long hesitation.

"More like good afternoon," said the patch-eyed man.

Richon nodded agreeably and turned away, thinking that would be the end of it.

But he had miscalculated.

"What's a man like you doing here?" The patch-eyed man waved at Richon's finely made clothes, improved by his recent bath. "Spying for the king?" He laughed.

Richon felt his heart skip a beat, then pasted a sickly smile on his own face. Surely this man had never seen the king before. It was only a joke.

The drunken man mumbled a few words, then said more clearly, "Always pretending he had no magic, though we all know it's not true."

The owner of the alehouse noticed Richon and came over to him. "What will it be, then?" he asked.

"Ale," said Richon, remembering how he had always had that when he was already well and truly drunk.

He turned back to the patch-eyed man. "You think the king has magic?" His throat was so tight he could hardly get the words out.

The patch-eyed man shrugged. "We all of us have magic, every one. It is only a matter of how much or how little."

"Surely there are exceptions," said Richon, drawn into the conversation despite himself.

The patch-eyed man shook his head. "If they live and breathe, they have magic, big or small. Those who think otherwise haven't looked deep enough."

Richon was annoyed. Was this man saying that anyone who had no magic just had not tried hard enough to find it? He was a man who had lived two hundred years and more. He knew what he had—and what he did not.

"Some say it's those who have the strongest magic who hold it back the most," said the patch-eyed man.

"They're afraid of it, see," the drunken man broke in, his words slow but clear. "Afraid of how much bigger it is than they are. And how it will change them."

Well, that might be true of others, but it wasn't true for Richon. He felt sure of that.

"Knew a woman like that once," the drunken man said.

The patch-eyed man said, "He's known plenty of women, but not recently, eh?" He smiled and made a rude gesture.

But Richon was impatient. "What happened to her? The woman you knew?"

"She died," said the drunken man. "But she had at last found her magic. Took her sixty-eight years of life, but when she found it, oh, how strong it was!"

"Why did she die, then?" asked Richon.

"When she realized her magic, she saw how all her life she had done nothing for the animals around her. As a recompense, she joined with the wild man."

"She was the hawk who did as the wild man bid, against the king," said the drunken man. "She died of an arrow wound in the final battle. Killed by her own people, trying to save them from the king who hated magic."

The hawk, thought Richon. He had a flash of memory of that hawk. The dark eyes, the flapping wings, the intense glare.

But he had not noticed the hawk dead of an arrow wound on the battlefield.

The truth was, he had not noticed any of the animals who had died. They had been no more than animals to him then.

Richon took another sip of his sharply flavored drink, very different from the ale from the palace. But he realized he was no longer here for oblivion. He was here to learn of magic, and found himself hoping as he had always refused to hope before.

"Tell me how you use your magic," he said to the patch-eyed man.

He shrugged. "To call to the birds to get away from my field so as to have more food to harvest come fall. To walk through the forest and call out to the wolves to leave me be. To give the mice one loaf of bread to eat through a month's time instead of watching them take bites of each loaf as it's fresh from the oven."

He turned to Richon, suspicious once more. "You don't use your magic for such as that?"

Richon shook his head.

The patch-eyed man stood up. "You think you're better than we are and won't use your magic on ordinary things?"

"No, no," Richon said.

But the patch-eyed man put up his fists and threw one at Richon's face.

Richon flew several feet across the room and fell, crumpling a chair behind him.

He groaned.

The alehouse owner ran toward him, clucking his tongue. "Sir, let me help you up. Shall I find you a room? Do you need a physician?"

Richon was bleeding from a cut on the face.

He was stunned.

He did not know whether to think of it as a prize or an insult that at last he had been treated as a man rather than a king.

The patch-eyed man stood, finished the rest of his drink, and wiped his mouth with his sleeve. "Let's leave this wretched place," he said to the drunken man.

"Yes, go, go," said the alehouse owner, bending over Richon once more.

Richon struggled to his feet. He wanted to call the

other two men back. There was so much more they could tell him.

But then the drunken man took a step toward Richon.

"The great magics come latest," he said. "And are most hidden. But they will out." He nodded to Richon, then stumbled out.

Suddenly Richon found himself thinking of the royal steward, who had seemed to have no ear for music. He hated the sound of it, and was always complaining about the noise. He had not the power to ban it, but he often chose to absent himself from occasions where music would be playing unavoidably—dances, plays, tales sung by bards.

Yet Richon remembered a woman who had once played the harp at the palace. She had called to the royal steward and played a special song for him. It had not sounded particularly beautiful to Richon, but the royal steward was moved beyond words. It brought tears to his eyes and made him tremble so that he could not even sit on a chair.

"What happened?" Richon had asked, staring at the woman and at his steward.

"He has a sensitive ear for music," said the woman.

"He hates music," Richon insisted.

"No," said the woman. "I have seen his like before. He only hates music that is not perfect. Absolutely perfect. And even of those who play music well, so few can play it perfectly. He has simply never had a chance to hear perfect music before. But now he has."

Richon watched as the royal steward struggled to regain control of himself. Eventually he had made his way to his own chambers, though Richon had heard nothing from him for the rest of the night and much of the following day.

The woman with her harp had gone the next morning.

At last, when the royal steward had emerged, Richon asked if he should have kept the woman there, to offer more of her unique sounds.

But the royal steward had shaken his head, speaking as if to himself—for he had never been so open with Richon before. "Never again. It unmanned me very nearly," he said quietly. He motioned to the place where the woman had sat, playing the harp. "She seemed to think it a gift in me that I could feel it so deeply and so rarely. But to me it seems more of a curse."

Richon had thought he understood then. The royal steward had gone on as he always had, avoiding music whenever he could.

As for the woman with the harp, she had come to the palace some months later and offered to play again.

Richon went privately to the royal steward, but his answer then was the same as it had been the day the woman had left.

"I am not myself with that music playing," said the royal steward, his teeth tightly clenched.

Richon had sent the woman on her way and given her

a fine purse in return for her offer to play. But he also asked her never to come to the palace again.

"Ah, he is afraid of it," the woman had said, nodding sadly. "I can see that. Those who are used to denying it can sometimes never learn to appreciate it fully. Well, I pity him."

Richon had never understood why she might do so, until now.

CHAPTER TWENTY-NINE

Chala

AFTER RICHON HAD disappeared into the ale-house, Chala found herself drawn toward a horse and hound tied together at a post on the other side of the street. It seemed a strange pairing.

She walked closer, then bent down to put a hand out to the hound, and the hound licked her hand dutifully, but did not so much as bark at her, though she was a stranger.

Was it simply well trained?

There was something very restrained in all its motions. Chala had never seen a hound, even a tame one, that looked around so little or seemed to have so little sense of play.

She found a stick on the ground and threw it.

The hound did not even follow the falling stick with its eyes.

She drew closer and sniffed the hound. It was not—right. There was a very flowery human perfume lingering on the hound's fur, the residue of a recent bath, but she was not sure that was all.

She let a hand run across the hound's back.

It was dark brown with white on its belly, as were many of the hounds in the forests to the south even in her own time.

She looked around herself to make sure there were no humans nearby, then barked an inquiry in the language of the hounds. "Meat?" she asked, thinking that any hound would perk up at that word.

But this hound turned to her with a blank expression and then turned back.

So, it was a tame hound, one that had given up its own language for the language of humans.

She put out her hand again, let it be licked, and said, "Good boy," in the language of humans.

But the hound had no more response to this than it had to her speaking in the language of the wild hounds. Nor could it be deaf, because it had looked toward her on her first approach.

What was wrong with it, then?

She gave it a piece of the journey cake that Richon had bought several villages past.

The hound licked the cake from her hand and then hung its head once more.

Chala turned to look at the horse.

There was something in its stance that reminded her of the hound.

Horses were animals that did not give up their own language, even once they were tamed by humans. She had never tried to speak in the language of horses before, but she trusted her new magic and tried it. She stroked the horse's dappled gray and white neck while saying—she hoped—"Cool weather, good rest."

She looked up at the horse afterward to see its reaction. Would it think she was a complete fool for speaking so haltingly?

But the horse did not look at her at all. It was as if she had said nothing.

Chala tried it again.

And then she tried other words. She offered the horse a piece of the journey cake, but the horse did nothing until she held the cake out in her hands and toward its nose. Then it turned toward the food and nibbled at it.

The perfumed scent from the hound had spread to the horse, or perhaps they had been washed together. But there was another scent. Chala was sure of that. She put one hand on the horse and one on the hound and concentrated.

As soon as she realized the truth, she leaped away from both of them, cold fear twisting around her spine.

The unmagic.

It had infected them both, though it was not as virulent as the variety in the forest, and left both animals

living—after a fashion. They were more than domesticated, as humans had been doing with animals for
centuries. These animals had been stripped of any sense
of their own lives. They had no will of their own. They
were not even animals anymore, but lumps of clay that
moved when told to by a human.

It made her sick.

At that moment a man came out of one of the houses
and nodded to her. He stood on legs that bowed, as if
he spent most of his life on horses, and he had a well-
trimmed beard and mustache.

He nodded to the horse, smiling widely. "The gentlest
horse you ever saw, isn't it?" he asked.

"Very gentle," Chala admitted.

"And the best-trained hound to be found anywhere."
He clapped his hands and the hound lay down obediently,
all four legs tucked under him, head bowed as if before
a king.

"Do you have need for one or the other—perhaps both?
My lady, I assure you that you have come to the best animal tamer in the kingdom." His smile never wavered.

Chala stared openmouthed at him. He thought what
he was doing was taming? Did he not see the difference
himself? He had the unmagic in him, and he used it and
called it taming. What a fool he was.

But a dangerous fool!

"Or perhaps you have a horse of your own that is too
much for you? Won't come when it's called or bites your

226

men and other horses in the stables? Ruins equipment and has a nasty temper? I have dealt with all of those and they are no problem for me."

Chala stayed where she was, listening for any information the man could give her about what he did and where he had learned it—or from whom. With every word, she became more sickened. The man was proud of how he had transformed these animals into stones that moved. He thought humans would want animals this way, and Chala realized he must be right. He would not still be in business if there were not some humans who wanted this.

Did they not taste the unmagic? Or did they not care?

The man patted the dappled horse's back. "You would not recognize this horse from the one that I bought two months ago from a merchant going north. He tried to ride him and was ready to shoot the beast, but I came along and offered a few copper pieces. He was glad to take them and warned me I'd be wasting my feed if I kept her alive. But it worked well enough for both of us, didn't it, Sweet?"

Why could humans not accept that there would always be some animals that could not be tamed, because they would not accept the exchange of one language for another or give up the forest for a human pasture?

"Could you explain what you do?" asked Chala, pretending interest. "It seems such a wonder for you to change a horse so radically in just a few months. A horse whose character has already been determined in a young life. Is it your strength alone?"

The man lifted a gloved hand to Chala. "It's in this," he said.

"What?"

He took off the black leather glove and Chala held it to her nose.

There it was—the smell of the unmagic. The smell that was underneath the perfume on the hound and the horse. The smell that she'd had too much of in the first moment she'd noticed it. And this man smiled at it!

"Where did you get this?" Chala asked carefully.

The man seemed eager enough to talk. "It came to me when I was a young boy. Lucky thing, too, for my parents were poor farmers and I would have had to live on their farm for the rest of my days, growing plants and hunting in the forest for meat. They did not even have animals to raise until I began to take them from the forest with me."

Chala shivered, but forced herself to go on with the charade. She spoke casually. "I met a man who was like you once, from the south. He had the same ability to gentle animals. He had a certain striping around his nose."

"Oh?" said the man, his smile faltering.

Was it possible the cat man was in this time, as well? If so, Chala did not know how to find him.

"So, shall I sell this animal to you? One gold coin?"

the man asked, his smile pasted on once more.

"No," said Chala, shaking her head. She had magic but did not know if she could help a horse changed like this. It was not at all the same as helping Crown. What would be left of this horse if the unmagic were stripped from it?

"A silver coin, then," said the man, interpreting Chala's reluctance as an invitation to bargain. When she did not answer immediately, he nodded to the hound. "I will give you this hound as well. It's as fine and gentle as the horse, I assure you. Fetches and follows commands without a word, and it won't even whine when you eat and it goes hungry."

Chala's heart ached at this description, and she had to turn her head and walk away.

Still, the man called after her.

"Five copper pieces, then. Or you can come with me and I'll show you some others. I have plenty to choose from. I only brought these because a man here wished to see them, though now he says he has already bought others."

It was all Chala could do to walk away. She vowed that this man and the unmagic here would be dealt with later, after the battle.

CHAPTER THIRTY
Richon

THOUGHTS OF MAGIC whirled in Richon's head. Magic was everywhere, in every Eloliran.

He found Chala standing near a hound, a horse, and a man who seemed to own them.

He nodded absently toward Chala and ignored the others. He simply picked up the sack of swords he had left beside her and moved toward the end of the town.

"How was your drink?" asked Chala, on his heels.

"Fine," said Richon shortly. He knew he should explain to her what had happened, but he had to sort it out in his own head. He was still not sure he believed it.

"You look unsteady," she said.

He was indeed. He tripped over his own feet, stumbling into Chala and nearly pulling her down.

She stared at him with disgust. "You are drunk," she said.

"No," said Richon. He had only had the one drink.

"At least, not on ale. It was . . ." He could not say it out loud. Not yet.

Chala walked with him, but not so close anymore that he might walk into her.

Moving out of the town, they passed a well. She stopped to drop a bucket in and dumped it on top of her head.

He watched as the water poured down her face.

Then she did the same thing again. And again.

The fourth time, she rubbed her hands in the water, and failing to find soap, used a stone nearby to make her hands raw.

"What are you doing?" he asked, torn out of himself for a moment.

"Making myself clean," she said.

Was she that disgusted by his drinking?

He wanted to tell her he had magic, as she did. But if he was wrong— He dared not give her, or himself, hope that was false.

They walked farther, and Richon wondered if every person they passed had magic.

Had his whole court had magic and simply hidden it from him all those years?

His own body servants?

The cook?

The stable boys?

Lady Finick and Lady Trinner?

The lord chamberlain?

The royal steward?

And himself?

Was it possible that a man could have magic for more than two hundred years and not know it?

He had wanted the magic so often it had eaten at him. But he had never been able to find the least stirring of it inside himself.

Even now he had come to save those with the magic, not to find his own.

And besides, those who had magic needed no lessons in it. It simply came to them, like crawling or walking upright.

Chala put a hand on his shoulder and turned him around to face her. "You must listen to me. The unmagic is here in this time as well. I have seen it, in the forests, and elsewhere."

"Elsewhere?" Richon echoed, turning to her.

"The horse and the hound in the village. They were touched by unmagic." She shuddered. "Made lifeless."

"Unmagic? And I did not sense it?" Was that not proof enough that he had no magic? "Should we go back?"

"No. We must first save the kingdom. Then we can save its magic."

They walked on, and Richon thought of one day when he was a child and he had found his mother standing under a parasol outside the palace, dressed in her night-clothes, her hair still tied back in braids, though it was the middle of the day.

"I am thinking," she said when he asked her what she was doing.

She did not look at him or turn toward him as she always had before. She did not give him her full attention.

It seemed she was deeply herself in this moment, and not his mother. Or his father's wife. Or Elolira's queen.

"What are you thinking of?"

"I am not thinking of anything. I am thinking," she had said.

So he had tried to do the same. Think, but not of any particular thing. Just think.

He had run away after trying it for just a moment or two. It had been like drowning. He could not breathe. He could not even tell where he ended and everything else began. There were no boundaries, and he needed boundaries.

Now he found himself slipping away from his own sense of self. It was not so hard, nor so frightening, as it had been when he was young. He drifted in his mind and was no longer tethered to his body. He did not know if he was still walking with Chala or if he had stopped.

It did not matter.

He felt as if he were touching tender new skin to the world around him, and the sensations were exquisitely clear and sharp. Everything touched him.

The forest. The sounds of the animals within, the tiny flutter of leaves, the burble of a stream nearby, the smell of life and death combined, of wildflowers and juniper bushes, the sight of color juxtaposed on color, green overwhelming all.

He quickly became exhausted by the overwhelming sensation, but there was no escape. The magic, long put off, had come for him at last, and it pressed at him with demands such as he had never known.

It was as if his ears had grown larger, for he could hear the scurry of the ants searching for food in the rotting limbs of a tree, and the beetles with them, the worms in the ground underneath, digging their way through dirt.

His nose was overwhelmed with scents, as when he was a bear. The scent of berries. A dead mouse, rotting in the leaves. The fish in the stream. Overhead, the scent of an owl's nest.

He could see to the woodpecker's marks on the oak tree there, and the lines left in the dirt by the crossing of a snake.

His hands felt as if they were on fire from the feel of the air on them, telling him so many things. Speaking to him in a new language.

And he tasted the whole world. Flowers yet to bloom. Pine trees far away in the mountains. The meat a mother wolf fed her cub.

He choked and gasped.

In his mind he heard a sound, soft and high-pitched as his mother's voice, but something else altogether. It was inviting, and he stepped into a new place that was full of all the sensations he had felt before, only they did not overwhelm him. They were part of him, but not all of him.

He felt his body again.

He was slumped against a log, and Chala was next to him.

He turned to her and now he could see the magic in her. The color was green, and it pulsed through her like blood.

He could see the magic everywhere now, in all the animals around him. Even the trees had a portion of magic, though it was a cooler green. The air itself, it seemed, was made of life, for it, too, had a greenish tinge to it.

What else could he see?

He looked down at his own hands and saw the magic in them.

If he had needed more proof, here it was. His hands were so bright that they were more white than green. He stared at them, feeling part of the forest as he had never felt before.

It was like falling, and yet he fell into himself.

He heard a sound from Chala.

She pointed to his hand, on his knee.

He glanced toward it and saw a bear paw on his knee rather than the human hand he had begun with. Only one bear paw, and it was fading quickly, becoming smaller and hairless, losing its claws.

But still, there it had been.

And he had changed it himself, not the wild man.

"Your magic," said Chala encouragingly.

It made him immediately want to try again.

But by then he had a terrible headache that seemed to block his vision entirely. The world was black again, with floating blobs of light in it, all color gone.

He banged on the doors of his mind, but it was no use.

The magic had suddenly fled him, like a fish avoiding his grasp as he leaned over a pool of water, eager for dinner.

"It will return when you are ready," Chala assured him as he held his head to his knees, afraid that if he did not he would fall to pieces.

But he told himself that Chala was right as he held her in his arms, and for the first time he felt he might be worthy of her.

CHAPTER THIRTY-ONE
Chala

T HEY SPENT THE night in the forest. In the morning when Chala woke, she was next to the bear.

She reached out a hand and touched him.

He started, growled, and then sat up.

She waved at his bear form.

Richon—the bear—looked at himself and then closed his eyes.

Chala watched then as he slowly transformed himself from bear into man. Slowly, without the ease the wild man might have used, but steadily and without doubt.

"I have often wondered why the wild man did not change me into something smaller and more disgusting, rather than a bear," said Richon. "If I was to learn what it was like to be an animal, one who was hunted instead of the hunter, he could have made me a hare or a possum or some other creature that could not defend itself easily in a forest full of larger predators."

"Perhaps he did not want you to die quickly," said Chala.

Richon looked at Chala. "What if that was not the reason, either?"

Chala did not understand.

"What if it was my own magic, working unknown to me?" asked Richon.

"And you chose to live for two hundred years as a bear?" asked Chala. "You were so miserable, were you not?" For all those years he had been utterly alone.

"Yes, but I had not finished something. I could feel that. I thought it was the wild man, saying that I had not yet learned my lesson. But if it was my magic all along, then it was my sense of incompleteness, not his, that kept me living."

"Without knowing it," said Chala.

Richon nodded. "Do you remember," he added. "When we went to the wild man, he said that I had to choose. He said that it was my choice if I went back as a king. What if he meant that it was my magic that would transform me, as it had at first?"

"And mine?" asked Chala. "He said that it was my choice, that you could not stop me."

Richon stared at her wonderingly. "Do you think all animals have the magic, then?" he asked. "In this time as well as in the future?"

"I think so, yes," said Chala. All living things seemed to have it, though as the unmagic grew, it seemed to grow more faint, in both animals and humans.

"But do they know it? Did you know it before you came here?"

"No," Chala admitted. She thought of the animals in her dream. Had they known they were using the magic?

Certainly animals in her own time did not know they had magic. It was easier now, when the feel of it was all around, rich and sweet, to discover it inside.

"So, the magic is there in us," said Richon wonderingly, "whether we know of it or not. It is part of us."

"Or are we part of it?" asked Chala.

"Yes," said Richon, half smiling. "The closer you are to magic, the more difficult it is to draw the line between what is magic and what is not."

"But what does this have to do with you being made into a bear?" asked Chala.

"I think when the wild man changed me, he drew from what was already inside of me to make me a bear. That was my natural shape, for some reason. I am at heart a bear."

Chala thought of the family of shape changers they had met before. All had chosen to be hounds. She had thought at the time that it was purely a matter of safety, for it was less conspicuous to travel as a pack of wild hounds than as five different animals.

Perhaps they had all been hounds because that was simply the way they were.

And the children in the animal race had each had

239

his or her own form and seemed unable to change to another.

She thought of humans she had known when she had been a princess. There had been Lord Sniff. At least that was what she had always called him in her mind. He was always sniffing his nose at things, as if that were the only way to make a judgment. It had been very like a cat, and she had told herself that was part of the reason she had disliked him, for hounds and cats can never live together happily.

And King Helm. She had thought of him with a boar's head on top of his large, muscled human body. He was as tough as a boar, and she had respected him for that, but he was also as difficult to reason with as a boar, as intent on only one thing: the battle.

The woman with the long neck who had always looked at herself in mirrors like a swan was Lady Torus. She had had a long nose, and long fingers, almost like wings.

And Prince George? A rabbit, perhaps. But a strong one, who was unexpectedly victorious against those far larger because of his great magic.

"Last night I thought of the magic and whether I would ever be able to use it again," said Richon. "Then, when I slept, I watched the eagles fly, and I envied them. But I could not transform myself into their shape. I watched the fish swim, and no matter how I concentrated I could not make myself into a fish. But when I tried to make myself into a bear, it came so easily."

"And the language of the bears? Why could you never speak that?" asked Chala.

Richon sighed. "Perhaps I did not want to. That would be admitting the truth of all of this, which I could not face." He made a wide gesture with his hands that took in the whole forest, the whole kingdom, and beyond. "The magic, and who I was."

"You must be a very stubborn man," said Chala.

Richon laughed. "I thank you," he said with a short bow. "I will take that as a compliment, coming from a very stubborn woman—and hound."

Chala thought.

"Can I change back into a hound, then, too?" she asked quietly.

But she already knew the answer. She had been a hound in the dream that was not a dream.

She looked at herself. Her human legs, under the long red skirt, her human feet, encased in boots. Human hands, roughened and callused as they had been from the first—because she was not a woman who looked for an easy life, any more than she was a hound who did the same. Human hair, black and thick, warm as her hound's fur. Human hips, to keep her feet separated in a wide, strong stance that would not yield.

"Close your eyes," said Richon.

Chala closed her eyes.

"Do you feel the magic within you?" Richon asked.

"Yes," said Chala.

Richon gave a short laugh. "Then you are already ahead of me. To feel the magic was most of the work for me. Now you must simply see yourself in the form you wish and the magic will make it come to be."

Chala thought of how she saw herself now as a hound and a woman. Not as only one or the other. But what made her feel most like a hound?

She let out a snarl, a hound's sound, and thought of how it had felt before, when she had thought it was the wild man changing her.

She snarled again, and then leaped—

Before she landed she was in the form of a hound once more.

It felt so good. She put her head to the ground and chased after the smell of a badger.

Richon ran with her as a bear, and ate what she ate. She shared with him what she could share with no other: the joy of being human and being animal. If she could change from one to the other, perhaps she would not feel such a loss as she had feared. She could be a hound when it was right to be a hound and a human when that was necessary. She might not fit with others, but she would always fit with Richon.

When they were finished eating, the hound became Chala once more, and the bear Richon.

"I think it is just as well that I did not know of the magic before," said Richon. "I shudder to think how I would have used it when I was a boy."

"Perhaps if you had had it, it would have made you different," said Chala.

Richon shrugged. "Well, that is neither here nor there. What matters is who I am now, and how I can use this magic to save my people and the generations to come."

It was such a houndlike thing to say that for a moment Chala was speechless. Then she laughed.

She and Richon changed forms as it was useful to them over the next few days, cutting across fields, over rocky barriers, moving ever closer to the battlefield ahead.

They both returned to human form at the entrance to a large forest. There was something wrong about it. It smelled of decay—and worse.

Chapter Thirty-two

Richon

T HE FOREST WAS darker than any Richon had ever been in, and older. The trees were enormous, their canopies high overhead, and their leaves were so thick that little light trickled below. This forest was near the edge of Elolira. The greenery here was more like that of the southern kingdom of Nolira, so he knew he was close to the battlefield. He heard no sounds, however—no calling of birds overhead, no chittering of possums under the tree boughs, no hopping of rabbits underfoot. It was unearthly still.

Yet there was something calling to him, almost a physical force pulling him forward, tugging at his chest so that the swords moved uncomfortably against his shoulder bones.

He turned to look at the hound and saw that she was unsettled, too.

They went deeper into the forest and slowly smelled

the stench of the cat man's unmagic ahead, worse than ever before.

With each step Richon was sure that he could go no farther, that this had to be the worst of it. But always he could feel more of the unmagic ahead, and so he went on and on. They came at last to the center of it.

It was at the top of a small hill, in a clearing about the size of Richon's own palace courtyard. There was no green here at all, and when Richon looked inside of himself to see with his other eyes, he could see no light, no color—nothing.

But it was not empty of form, though it was empty of magic.

There were animals here, hundreds, perhaps thousands of them, all lying together, stretched out, dead, their bodies blackened as if burned. They had not sunk into the earth as the animals had in the future, when the unmagic had spread into the forest and the bear had only just had time to save the fawn. Somehow the bodies were untouched by the unmagic all around them. And Richon could touch the ground around them without being sucked into the unmagic himself. In their death they had left behind protection.

Though the bodies did not stink, Richon was sure they had been dead for some time. There was no vegetation around them, no insects crawling over them, no flies overhead, no buzzards coming toward the smell of death—because there was no smell. Except for the smell of the unmagic itself.

Richon bent down, then fell to his knees, unable to stay upright, unable to stop his weeping.

All of these creatures, dead.

Just as in the future, he had failed to save them from the unmagic.

Richon rose. He took deep, gasping breaths and forced himself to walk through the clearing. He looked at each carcass, hoping to find some clue as to what had happened to them and how the unmagic had not completely dissolved their forms.

They were with their own kind. The shrews with shrews, the foxes with foxes, the bears with other bears. The crows had all fallen together, and next to them were other birds: eagles, hawks, sparrows, finches, robins, and jays.

Richon moved back out to stand at the edge of the clearing. Chala stood by him, as silent as the ancient forest itself.

Richon closed his eyes, as if to use his magic to help him, but he could sense nothing. Whatever life the animals had once had, it was gone now, erased as if it had never been. Yet all had been together, called for a united purpose.

Richon groaned as the truth struck him.

It had only been weeks since the wild man had called to the animals in Richon's kingdom to fight against him.

Richon had never thought what might have happened to those animals once the battle was over and he had been turned into a bear.

It seemed they were here, many of them.

They had been caught together by one who wielded unmagic and turned the strength of their combined magic against them.

And this, too, was Richon's fault.

The only question that remained in his mind was why their bodies had not yet decayed. Richon could feel no magic around them, but he could not see why the unmagic would not have turned them to gray dust.

He looked for Chala, and then saw her as a hound, walking through the ranks of the fallen wild hounds. She stopped in front of each carcass and gave out a howl of mourning.

Richon had never known a human woman who could have faced something like this. And she did not stop with the hounds. She moved to the other animals, body by body, and howled for them as well. She seemed to go through them in order of those most like the hounds. Wolves, then porcupines, sables, wolverines, and stoats, and, last of all, the birds. Richon followed after her, looking at each animal, fixing the image of their forms in his mind, holding them there with magic and giving them names in his mind. Not their own names, perhaps, but names nonetheless.

Here was a family of caribou, the father buck with a great rack on his head at the front, the mother behind him, and the child standing behind them all. All dead in the same moment, with no chance for one to protect another, but a family nonetheless.

CHAPTER THIRTY-THREE

The Hound

HER THROAT HAD never felt so rough. She had torn it with howl after howl, not giving herself a moment's rest. It had been the one way she could think of to make things better for these animals who had been killed by unmagic.

"We should go now, I think," said Richon as the morning light grew hot. There was no cool breeze here, as if the wind itself were afraid to come through the trees of this forest.

The hound hung her head, taking in great gulps of air. She wondered if she would ever feel whole again. She felt the deaths of these animals as if they were her pack, and the pain of their loss tore at her more because a part of her was human and did not see death as natural and inevitable.

In any case, these deaths had not been natural, any of them.

Suddenly there was a streak of sunlight from over-head, and the hound felt the descent of something heavy from above.

Rain?

She looked up and saw nothing, but felt the same sense of weight approaching.

Richon saw it, too, and reached for her.

The weight—whatever it was—was falling slowly. And it was warm.

Then the hound gasped as she realized what it was.

Magic!

And it belonged to the animals. She could sense it as it descended toward them.

This was why their bodies had not disintegrated.

The unmagic had caught them unawares. They had not had time to flee. But they could have fought back. They could have thrown their combined power against him, but they had chosen not to.

For if they had, their magic would have been swallowed up. And it was wrong for that magic to be gone from the world.

Though none of these animals had any hope of giving their magic to a son or a daughter, to a mate or a cousin, or even to any of their own species, the hound realized, they had wanted to keep it safe. And so they had sent it up into the air above them, still attached to their forms but away from the greedy unmagic, waiting for magic to call to magic.

The magic of a thousand animals or more—it was hot and heavy, and very sweet.

The hound did not think it was for her.

She turned to Richon, who held out a hand, as if reaching for the magic. Then he pulled back and looked at her.

"I am the last man who should take it. The very last. I am the cause of their death, and they hated me. They must have, to fight against me as they did."

He stared at the hound, his eyes wide and red, his hands clenched into fists.

The stance of a man ready to do battle, thought the hound. It reminded her of King Helm.

"There are humans who died because of you and yet you still think yourself able to be their king. How is this different from that?" she asked simply. Perhaps it was a hound's argument, but it was true for humans as well.

"Because I was born to be a king of humans. Not of animals," protested Richon.

"Both," the hound barked at him. It was never as easy to speak as an animal. The words were simply not as complex. But the hound felt it would be wrong to change back into a human now, and Richon could understand her in either tongue.

Richon took in a choking sob. "I have another battle to fight first." He looked out to the southern edge of the

251

forest, beyond which his army was supposed to be, battling other humans who threatened his kingdom.

"There is only one battle," the hound barked. "And one magic."

At last Richon lifted his head to the magic, as if welcoming it. He spread out his arms. And then he opened himself.

The hound could feel the block he had been using to press against the magic simply disappear, and the magic flowed into him naturally. Then she saw him sag, and put a hand to his mouth, as if to stop himself from vomiting the magic back up.

He took a tottering step. Then steeled himself and took another.

"They trust me," he said, half in wonder, half in despair. "I may do whatever I wish with their magic. They give me free rein."

The hound was not surprised. She, too, trusted Richon to the end of her life and beyond.

But she turned back to the animals one more time and saw that the bodies, held lifeless but untouched by death, had changed. They had begun to melt into the ground, overcome by the unmagic now that their magic had been taken up by Richon.

In a few hours' time there would be nothing left to mark this spot except a vast field of cold death. The animals would be erased entirely, as the cat man must have intended from the beginning.

CHAPTER THIRTY-FOUR

Richon

RICHON COULD HEAR the sounds of the battle at the border of Elolira and Nolira as soon as he stepped out of the ancient forest and the hound changed into human form at his side. It had been more than two weeks since he had passed back through the gap into his own time, and he had been preparing for this all that time. Even so, it seemed to take him by surprise.

The clanging of swords, the cries of death, the rearing of horses as they trampled foot soldiers. And the call of generals who were far back from the actual fighting. It was familiar and yet Richon had never been so afraid. He had never cared so much about the outcome.

"You should stay back," he said to Chala. "Here, where it is safe." He nodded to the edge of the forest.

"Safe?" said Chala. "When I have faced the unmagic time and time again already?"

"But this is different," said Richon. "You will not be fighting with magic here."

"No, I will not. Give me a sword," said Chala, nodding to the sack he carried. "I will fight with that."

"You?" said Richon.

She stared him down. "Do you forget that I was a princess once, and that the princess had a father who was a warrior first and foremost?"

"But surely he did not train you," said Richon.

"No," said Chala. "He did not. But that does not mean I did not train. It was in secret, but it was one of the few things that I liked about having a human body even then. A hound has no way to manipulate a weapon—and no need to do it, either.

"But I liked the strength that I felt when I swung a sword. It was the one way that I could be in a hunt without having to make an excuse to leave for the forest."

Richon was tempted to give her a sword just to satisfy his desire to see her holding it, fire in her eyes, her breath coming swift and deep in her chest. A human woman with a hound's heart.

"Did King Helm ever allow you to battle on the field— with men?" asked Richon.

"No," admitted Chala.

Richon nodded. "Because a woman would not be allowed in any army."

"Why not?" asked Chala. "If she is good enough, would they not welcome another warrior on their side?

It would be foolish not to."

Richon thought of all the reasons that he might give for this. The rules he had learned from boyhood. That a woman, no matter how strong, is not as strong as a man. That the male warriors would be distracted at the sight of a woman. That a woman in an army would cause the men to compete among themselves for her attention. That a woman simply did not belong on the battlefield—that her place was inside the walls of a palace, wearing fine clothes and drinking good wine while the men outside decided what flag she would swear allegiance to.

"Think of the last time you left me behind," said Chala. "And if you would do that again."

Richon burned at the memory. Chala had let him wound her very badly, and then had done what she wished to do anyway.

If he tried to do the same here, he did not doubt it would have the same outcome.

"If you do not wish me to be a woman in battle gear, I will be a hound. A bitch hound who hunts at the side of her mate," said Chala bluntly.

"You are not a bitch hound," said Richon. And he thought of her standing in his throne room. It was a revelation to him. Hound or human, she was the only queen he could imagine at his side.

Why had it taken him until now to realize that he loved her? That he had always loved her?

He had only been afraid of that love, and how deeply

he felt it. As afraid as he had been of his own magic. He had thought of how it would make him vulnerable, because he had felt the pain of loss before and knew how vulnerable he had been.

But love also made him strong. It made him strong enough to dare to take chances for himself, and for her.

"Come, then," he said at last. "However you wish to be."

"For this battle, then, a hound."

Then she bounded ahead of him, toward the clash of armies. He thought of the boy king he had been, and knew suddenly that even if he had known about his magic, even if he had been less selfish, he could not have faced this threat.

The wild man had had to let him learn, beyond what humans could learn in the few short years of life they had to them, in order to bring him here to counter this. He still did not know what he would do, but he knew now that he was capable. Two hundred years of life had brought him at last to the battle that his kingdom needed him to fight.

Coming around the hill, Richon recognized a voice calling out behind the soldiers, cursing them for their weakness, taunting them with insults to their wives and children.

It was the royal steward. Richon would have known that high-pitched scream anywhere.

Richon motioned for the hound to wait. He set the swords down, then went back to find a vantage point from which he could see the fighting well, and make a plan.

How many were in the invading army? Richon wished that he knew tactics better, but that had never been part of his training. His father had believed that diplomacy was the way to fight battles. And perhaps it usually was.

Not in this case, however.

Once again, Richon could see how his life as a bear had prepared him for this moment. It was not the same, of course, in tactics or strategy. But the mind-set was useful, the fierceness and the need for survival.

Richon made his way to the rocky outcropping above the battle. He crawled the last few feet toward the edge to keep his cover.

Then he stopped short and gasped.

This was no battle.

This was a slaughter.

Perhaps his men on the battlefield could not see it, but Richon could. They were hemmed in on all sides. There was no hope for victory. His men had little on them but dirty uniforms, some even in bare feet, but they fought against men in armor and boots.

Richon could see the royal steward watching it all, not calling retreat. The royal steward, who had insisted on the men having swords, but did not seem to care about any of the other rudiments of a fair battle between two armies.

Perhaps he had not had time to find such things. But

if that were the case, then his army should at least be falling back to better ground, to a better chance to fight again. But the royal steward was letting them die. Was he as incompetent as Richon was at battle? Or was there more going on here?

Richon watched more men die with each second, knowing that his hesitation had killed them. And yet his ignorance could kill even more.

He had to keep calm.

The hound was very quiet at his side. He did not doubt that she understood as much about this battle as he did, if not more.

He looked out over the field to the enemy troops. There were perhaps three thousand of them. Not an overwhelming number, though Richon could see only a thousand of his own men still standing. There were half that many dead on the field. And who knew how many days this battle had gone on?

Then Richon looked over at the horses standing behind the enemy lines. There was a very large man shifting frequently on one of those horses, standing back as the royal steward was standing back and with the same expression of watchful excitement on his face.

The lord chamberlain, the other man who had claimed to be his friend and adviser after his parents' death. Richon was sure it was him.

So, he sat on one side, and the royal steward on the other.

Were they truly on opposite sides or were they working together to make Elolira fall?

It did not matter.

One way or the other, his people were being sacrificed.

Richon could not allow it to continue.

CHAPTER THIRTY-FIVE

The Hound

T HE HOUND HAD never been the sort to stand by and watch a battle in progress, even if it had been no business of hers to begin with.

She remembered a time when she had come across a battle between a bear and a hound from another pack. She had had no obligation to the hound. It was simply that she knew that she might do something in the battle, and she itched to do it.

She had thrown herself at the bear's back, and sunk her teeth into its shoulder. The other hound had fled, but Chala had gone on for hours, fighting the bear until they were both senseless and exhausted. She had enjoyed it for the sheer beauty of the battle.

Richon was staring at the battle, twitching with each death, but not yet ready to throw himself in.

She did not wait. With a bark of regret, she leaped

over the rocks above the battle and down into the midst of it.

If it had ever been organized, it was so no longer. There were no lines of men standing together to hold back the enemy. Pockets of the enemy had penetrated nearly to the place where the hound landed. It was one man against another.

The hound snarled a warning—the kind of fair notice that animals and humans have in common. And then she opened her mouth, bared her teeth, and let them sink into the side of one of the Nolirans who held a sword in his hand.

He groaned, swatted at her, and then fell like a stone.

He must have been already weakened by battle and loss of blood. His face was very pale—for a moment.

Then the man he had been about to run through with his sword stood over him and took a battle-ax to his face.

The pale skin was spattered with blood.

The smell of it made the hound feel as though she were home again. But the human in her kept her from licking at it.

She turned away from the dead Noliran and saw three men directly ahead of her, two against one—and the one was Richon's man.

She was about to launch herself at one of the enemy's

chest when she heard a sound like rushing wind over-head. And a sound like a battle cry, but guttural, like an animal's.

It was Richon—in his bear form.

Like her, he must have decided that he could fight more fiercely as an animal.

She felt an intense pride—like what she had felt at the first sight of her daughter's birth—when she saw Richon's claws slash open first one man's chest and then another's face.

In two blows he had killed both men.

Or as good as killed them.

The man who had fought against them took a spear to the two chests to make sure they were dead, then moved on.

He seemed to see nothing amiss in the aid of a bear in his battle, nor did he show any fear that he might become the bear's next victim.

He had magic, thought the hound.

The bear turned to the hound, raising a paw as if in salute. They were together as animals now. She watched as the bear moved to the east, to try to shore up the defenses of the men there, who were letting far too many of the enemy through, deep into the soft underbelly of the Eloliran army. The hound noticed the enemy were still nowhere near the man who shouted orders from this side, the man whose voice had seemed to jolt Richon at the first screeching sound of it.

The hound leaped into the space between two men fighting and pressed hard into the legs of an enemy soldier so that he lost his balance. His arms flew up as he tried to catch himself.

It was enough.

He was dead.

She tried the same tactic a second time, but this time the enemy had seen her from a distance away and was not surprised. Instead he kicked at her, then stabbed Richon's man dead and turned his sword to her.

The hound stood her ground, daring him to try it.

He moved the sword quickly in a circle around her head.

As if that would make her afraid of him.

The hound wanted to laugh. She had seen these tricks from the very youngest of King Helm's soldiers. And the king had sworn at them and threatened them that they would not see another day with a sword, for he would kill them himself.

King Helm had had no patience with tricks. He had told his soldiers that if they wished to fight at his side, they had to give the best of themselves, for he was giving the best of himself. And if they died, they died in glory.

It had been one of the first times that the hound had understood a human point of view.

The sword circled again.

The hound simply ran from it, and turned to try herself at another pair.

As she ran, she heard the bear roaring at his own men to get out of the way, but few of them understood him. It was not because they had no magic, but because they were focused on another task—fighting for their lives.

Nonetheless, the hound and the bear moved from the back to the front of the line.

She cut open faces, gouged out eyes, and chewed at hands that held swords.

He cut heads open, tore off arms and shoulders, and crushed whole bodies.

At last, when it was nearly dark, the enemy army retreated, and so did the bear and the hound, scrambling back to the place above the battle where they had begun.

There they rested as dark fell, returning to human form.

Chala was exhausted as she had never been before and knew that only a human could push a body this far. A hound would simply have let the fight go, or let herself die. But she had fought on until she could hardly see.

"I should have saved more of them," said Richon as he looked out over the battlefield, which was at this point nearly invisible in the dark.

"Not just my own men, but those who fought them as well," Richon went on. "They were not evil. They were simply here to do what they had been sent to do. My father would have found a way to speak to them, to convince them to turn back. Somehow he would have used his magic to save lives. I have only made sure that the lives lost were someone else's."

Chala was surprised that she, too, felt a sense of loss at the deaths of her enemies. She had never felt such a thing as a hound.

CHAPTER THIRTY-SIX

Richon

THE SOUNDS ON the battlefield grew more muted. Richon leaned against Chala and wished he could lie down and close his eyes, and sleep until morning. But the work of the battlefield was not finished at night. Young boys pulled the dead to the sides and women and girls stripped them of uniforms and weapons, and whatever else they could find that was of use to the army. How many of the dead were their own relatives or friends?

With sudden determination to see the royal steward who had taken control of his army up close, Richon went back to the forest to retrieve the swords. He slung them back over his shoulder, except for one that he tucked into his tunic, for his own use.

Chala changed back into her hound form and followed him, but from a distance.

Richon kept his head down as he walked toward the

Eloliran army. He could hear shouts of pain from the tents of the physicians who worked to take off mangled limbs, sew entrails back into stomach cavities, and cauterize wounds oozing with infection.

"You there!" someone called to him.

Richon shuffled over.

"What are you doing here? Come to join the army?" It was a dark joke. Indeed, who would come to join this army, when it was losing so badly and the signs of death were everywhere?

"No," said Richon. He knew immediately that this was a man who had spent time with the royal steward. He held out the swords. "Came to bring these to the royal steward."

"Ah, good. We can always use more of those. I hope they're well made."

"Well enough made," said Richon. For the brute killing that was this war.

The man gestured to a tent.

It was lit from within and the strong scent of incense rose from it.

Richon kept his head low and moved toward the tent. Another guard stood in front, and Richon explained his errand a second time.

The guard offered to take the swords, but Richon shook his head.

"I've got to make sure they get to him. No offense. But it's my head," he said, gesturing upward. He tried to use the accent of the country rather than the more staid tones of the court, and to speak indistinctly.

The guard smiled and said, "Your head, eh? That it is." He laughed, and Richon pretended to laugh with him.

After a moment, the guard opened the flap to the tent and called within.

Then the royal steward stepped out.

The man seemed so much smaller than Richon remembered, and his face was twisted with anger.

Would the royal steward recognize him, ragged and covered in battle muck as he was?

But he hardly looked at Richon at all. "Yes?" he asked in an annoyed tone.

Richon held the swords out. "For you," he said roughly. "From the blacksmith in the village."

"Ah, yes. He works very hard for me. Now." The royal steward let out a tinkling laugh.

Once, Richon would have laughed along with him. Only a few weeks ago, as time flowed here. But Richon had changed.

"Well, you can go now. Hurry back to your safety, unless you want to stay here and show yourself a hero."

As a young king, Richon knew he had been blind and foolish. But the royal steward had no such excuse.

"I will stay," said Richon.

The royal steward snorted. "A hero, are you? Then stay you shall. Who am I to deny you your glory?" He nodded to the guard. "Take him to the food tent. And make sure he has a uniform. Must look right and proper for tomorrow." Sotto voce, he added, "When he dies."

Richon stiffened with anger.

It would take only one swipe of his bear's claws to tear the royal steward into pieces. But Richon did not want the man to die that way. He had caused such misery to so many, Richon must wait until the battle was over and there was order once more. Then he could make his judgment of the royal steward public, so all would see that the king did not support such behavior any longer.

The guard led Richon to a row of fires over which large racks of lamb were being roasted.

The tantalizing smell of the roasted meat in the food tent blocked out the other terrible smells in the camp. But few of the men seemed to be eating heartily.

Richon saw husbands and fathers, brothers and sons. These were his people, whom he had never bothered to see before.

After a few minutes, the guard tugged Richon away. "Then come get your uniform, if you're not hungry," he said.

He walked Richon to a clearing very close to the pile of the dead.

Richon cringed, not just at the multitude of death, but at the lack of respect shown the bodies of men who had given their lives for the kingdom. He wished he could do something for them.

Ahead, a man poked his head out of a tent. He was

balding, with a white mustache.

"A new uniform," said the guard.

"What? I've got no new uniforms." The man called out loudly. He was nearly deaf, it seemed.

"It will be new for him," said the guard, smiling grimly.

He left Richon there to be outfitted in a uniform with a slice through the chest and a terrible bloodstain that ran down the tunic and the trousers.

Richon shivered at the sight.

"He don't mind, you can be assured of that," said the balding man.

Richon nodded to him and dressed, but wondered if he would use the sword issued to him. He had never been much of a swordsman.

At last, he stepped out of the tent and stared back out over the dead. He had marked the faces of all the animals who had died in the forest for his sake. He could do no less for his own men.

He stretched for the words his father had given in the funerals he had presided over at court. They had always seemed the same, at least to a bored child dressed in stuffy, formal clothes, who did not care who had died, but wished to get on with his games.

He was no longer that child.

And he no longer felt bored at these deaths.

He ached with the weight of them.

Through that dark night, he bent over each of the

dead from that day, not yet piled up with the others. He touched a hand or brushed a cheek. He could not know their names or see their faces, but he could at least count them, as he had done with the animals who had died for him and given him what remained of their magic.

There were 2,668 dead.

The number was higher than he had ever counted before in his life. Yet he had done it carefully and slowly, so he had no doubt.

Richon felt the hound at his side and had a vivid flash of memory. His mother, walking beside his father, for once her constant smile gone. They had been at a funeral, and the tears they had shed had been real, though the dead were peasants in a faraway village who died in a rockslide.

Here was the hound—Chala—walking with him as his mother had once done, as a queen among her dead.

When Richon was done, the new day was dawning bright and beautiful, as if to insist that it was not a day for death.

A trumpet made the call to arms.

All around him Richon felt men rush forward into battle.

He wanted to go with them, and yet the more he tried to move, the more he felt frozen in place, as if a great weight were pressing on his chest, so he could hardly breathe.

He cried out, and even that sound was muted.

He tried to wave his arms, but they would not move.

The hound came closer and sniffed at him. She whined and put a paw on his chest.

With that, Richon began to search inside himself.

He heard animals, some cawing, some scratching, some growling, in a tumult, and he could not distinguish one voice clearly from another. Where had they come from? Why were they inside him?

Then he remembered the forest, and the magic he had taken into himself. It was there still, and the animals to whom it had belonged had somehow lodged in him as well.

The animals were clamoring for something, but it was not until Richon turned toward the pile of the dead that the sound became a roar.

And the animals inside him somehow began to tug him forward.

When he was standing close to the center of them all, he felt a warmth inside himself, and a sudden quiet.

His chest throbbed, as if his whole body were being stretched.

Then he felt an animal leap out of him. It was a great gray wolf. When Richon closed his eyes, he could see the green light of the wolf's magic, saved from the unmagic, in the midst of the dead.

Eyes open again, Richon could see one of the dead soldiers moving a foot.

For one moment Richon thought that the man had been set in the pile of the dead while yet living, and that he had struggled there for all these days, calling out, trying to show that he was not dead, and no one had seen him.

Richon felt horror at the thought.

And then he realized the truth.

The man had died.

But he was alive again. Because of the wolf.

The magic that gave life to all called the dead man back to his body and, combined with the strength of the animal's magic, had healed his wounds.

The hound barked wildly.

And the rest happened all in a rush, too quickly for Richon to tell the difference between one animal leaving him and one man rising out of the ranks of the dead.

The animals went to those men they had an affinity for, as far as Richon could tell. At least they did so where it was possible. A man who had always taken the form of a wolf would be stirred by a wolf; the same with a man who was an elk, or a mouse, or a fox in his animal form.

As Richon felt the magic pouring out of himself and into the dead, he felt that for the first time in his life he had done something right. Something only he could do. Something marvelous and magical.

This was what the wild man had set in motion from

the first, to make all of this possible. He could not help but weep, not at his own power, but at the chance he had been given to reclaim something of his life, to help others, animal and human both.

He watched in amazement as the world shifted around him.

As the sun rose, so did the dead, some of them naked because their uniforms had been stripped from them and given to another. Others were fully clothed, though bloody, and even still armed. Their faces came back to the color of life and they cried out in the language of animals and men combined as they ran forward into the battle. If their own comrades in arms were afraid of them, this was nothing compared to the reaction of the opposing army.

Magic was something both armies shared, to a degree. But to bring back the dead, with animal spirits to give them strength—that had never been seen before. It had never even been spoken of before.

There were not many brave enough to hold their ground, and even those who did so were soon over-whelmed. The battle that had seemed a slaughter to Richon yesterday was now a rout, on the opposite side.

It was not until Richon thought about the royal stew-ard that he realized there was no sign of the man, either at the front of the battle, with the men who were now fight-ing and winning, or at the back.

The royal steward's personal guards were in disarray,

some still standing where they had been the day before, the others joining in the fray. They were easy to spot— well-fed men with clean uniforms, terrified of those with magic.

The royal steward must have slipped away sometime during the battle, which he had meant to be a failure. To get his justice, Richon would have to go after him.

But for now there was the army of the King of Nolira before him. And then he saw the lord chamberlain on his horse, struggling to get clear of the battlefield.

Richon could not see his face, but slowly the small movements of the man in a panic removed all doubt. This was the lord chamberlain, who had seemed so kind, so gentle when he had come with the news of the deaths of the king and queen. He had made sure that Richon had time to himself, and was given sweets and hot drinks, anything that he asked for. Young Richon had not had to deal with the funerals at all. The lord chamberlain and the royal steward had done everything difficult for him.

And yet the two had hated each other. Richon had known that from the first, and now and again it had amused him to set them against each other. They would argue hotly until he sent them away. They only agreed on things that were to the advantage of both of them.

Each fought on a different side of this battle, but in the end they both must have wanted the same thing: the power of Richon's kingdom.

Richon shook with anger as he looked at the lord chamberlain across the field of battle.

Richon had lost the royal steward. But he would not lose the lord chamberlain as well.

CHAPTER THIRTY-SEVEN

The Hound

*S*HE HAD FOUGHT for a time as a hound, but she had stepped back for a moment to try to see where she should go next. Then she heard the odd sound of a tent coming down behind her, the cloth flapping in the sparse wind.

She turned and from a distance saw the royal steward, red-faced.

"No! I told you not to do that!" he cried.

"But you said to pack—" the young servant answered.

The royal steward struck him full across the face. "Do what I say or you will regret it."

"Yes, sir. Yes, sir," said the servant.

"Now put my things into a single pack that I can set on a horse. I want money and a change of clothes and a weapon. I need no more than that."

"But now that the battle is nearly won, surely you wish—"

The servant was struck again. "It is not your place to tell me what I wish and do not wish."

"I only meant—"

"Silence!" the royal steward thundered, far louder than the sound of his tent being struck, though nothing like as loud as the battle.

She remained a hound and watched. It was not much, perhaps, but she did it for Richon. This was a man he hated and would want to punish.

The servant went back into the folds of the tent and brought it back up on one end. He rummaged for a few moments, then came back out with a small pack. "Sir?" he said.

The royal steward opened the pack. "You did not think to add food to this? How long can I journey without food?"

"You did not say to—"

"Get food!" said the royal steward.

In the few moments before the servant returned, the royal steward had mounted a gray horse with a long tail, one the other horses kept away from.

The hound guessed why, but would have to confirm it.

The royal steward started off at a gallop, with no more concern for the horse than a bit of wood.

The hound bounded as fast as she could to keep up with the horse. Now she could see that it was very like the horse she had seen in the market. It, too, had been stripped of its magic. The creature that remained might look like a horse, but it was not a horse. Not in ways that mattered to other horses, or to the animal world at large.

So perhaps the royal steward was right to treat the horse so, and to not care if it was injured or even died from his mistreatment of it. Such a creature was better dead.

It rode on mindlessly, heartlessly. It did not think for itself. It simply was the creature that the royal steward demanded it be.

The hound could kill the royal steward for that alone. She shuddered in horror, and kept as close as she could without revealing herself.

After two hours at this punishing pace, she was exhausted. As a hound she had always considered herself the match of any horse, but the royal steward pressed his horse past its limits. He did not see it as living, and he did not care if it died. He could easily buy another. And if it was not one that had been touched by the unmagic, well, he would treat it as if it were.

Finally, the royal steward stopped at a village for food and water. The hound noticed that he tied his horse so that it could not graze. But it could drink from a dirty trough, at least, and it did so eagerly.

The hound drank from a clean trough and tried to find calm and strength in herself. She did not let herself doze.

Far too soon, the royal steward came out, looking well satisfied with his meal. He untied the horse and leaped back into the saddle, which he had never removed. He looked around once, as if expecting pursuers, then smiled and went on his way.

He had not looked down, only up, as if assuming that any who came after him would have to be mounted, as he was.

It was painful for the hound to run again after so short a stop. She told herself that if the royal steward stopped for the night, she would have a chance to take a kill. She had been far hungrier than this before and survived.

But she had never had to force herself to continue onward for so long at such a pace.

The hound could see the horse begin to miss steps, falter and correct itself. But the royal steward only swore at it and used a stick to urge it faster.

At last the horse fell and it did not get up.

The royal steward could see that he was not far from another village and that it was close to dark. He did not even bother to end the horse's life in a quick, decent fashion. He left it there to die slowly, in terrible pain.

The hound waited until the royal steward was out of sight.

She would find him again easily enough. It was clear that he would have to go to the village and rest for the night.

She bent next to the dying horse and tried to speak to it in the language of horses.

"I will help you along to the end," she said softly. If the horse did not understand her meaning, perhaps it would understand her tone.

But she could see no sign of any response in the horse.

The hound sighed, then bent close to the horse's neck, bared her teeth, and bit into it, severing its jugular vein. The taste of blood filled her mouth, and for the first time in her life she spat it out. She would not make herself stronger on the life of this creature. And she did not like the thought of the unmagic flowing into her. She did not know if that was possible, but she would not take any chances.

She waited until the horse was dead. Then she left its body where it was, and entered the village.

It was full dark now, but she could smell where the royal steward had walked. It was not only her tracking skills at work here, but also her sense of the unmagic. It was too clear a path to ignore. The hound only wondered that all the villagers did not notice it. But perhaps they did and did not care.

The trail of unmagic led to an inn at the other end of the village. It was small and dank, and one end of it seemed to be falling down. It was also very quiet, not at all the sort of place one would expect a man such as the royal steward to stay. Which made it a good hiding place, the hound supposed.

She heard voices within. One was the high-pitched, irritating, scraping voice of the royal steward. The other was lower—and familiar. It made her hackles rise even before she saw the face through the window staring back at the royal steward.

The cat man.

Here, in this time. Indeed, the path of unmagic she had followed to this inn was more likely the cat man's than it was the royal steward's.

The hound had to force herself to breathe again. The sight of the cat man in person was enough to make her vomit. But she had eaten nothing that day, so it was only dry retching.

When she was finished, she was trembling.

Truly she could not imagine anything more terrifying than the cat man. He had destroyed her forest home and it must have been he who had dribbled his unmagic throughout Richon's kingdom, destroying the animal army en masse.

Thinking of it made her feel cold, as if she herself had been touched by the cat man.

She had meant to attack the royal steward alone, to kill him and bring back evidence of his death to Richon, to show him he need worry about the man no more. Now her task had just increased a hundredfold. She did not know if she had any hope of destroying the cat man, but she knew she had to try.

Within the inn, she heard the royal steward and the

cat man laugh together, a terrible sound. And then she turned away and went into the woods to hunt.

She dared not go into the inn, as a human woman, and ask for food. She had no coin, and begging would draw attention she could not afford.

But she needed sustenance, and it would not hurt her to remember the violent rush of the chase, and the way that turned away fears.

CHAPTER THIRTY-EIGHT

Richon

RICHON RAN TOWARD the lord chamberlain, and justice.

By the time he reached him, the man had fallen off his horse and was trying desperately to get back on. All around him men were scrambling away from the battlefield, if they could still move. The ground was soaked with blood and there were dead Nolirans everywhere.

Richon called out to the lord chamberlain's horse in the language of horses.

"Away! Leave him and do not look back!"

The horse needed no more encouragement than that. He fled with the rest of the army.

The lord chamberlain gave a cry of despair, then turned and saw Richon approaching him.

He looked around, as if hoping to find help. But his guards had disappeared and left him to his fate. He turned back and put on a smile.

"King Richon, you cannot know how glad I am to see you!" he exclaimed, waving his arms widely as if that would distract Richon from the truth. "I thought that when the wild man had changed you into a bear you were gone forever."

"And so you turned to aid my enemy instead?" Richon asked.

The lord chamberlain swallowed, then stared at Richon. The spineless, foolish boy king he had last known had turned into a man.

"You misunderstand," he sputtered. "The royal steward—he took control of the armies. I knew that was not what you would want. He would have destroyed your kingdom, or if not that, taken it entirely for himself. Surely you noticed how power hungry he always was. When he saw the wild man turn you into a bear, he thought it was the perfect opportunity to take over your kingdom and crown himself. I had to stop that."

"Stop it by making yourself king instead?" asked Richon.

"No, no, Your Majesty. It was not for my sake. I only thought I would hold the kingdom for you until you returned. But I knew the royal steward would do no such thing." He was babbling, panicked enough that he was inadvertently letting truth spill out.

"Until I returned from being a bear?" asked Richon, his eyes narrowing. "What on earth made you think that

I would have the power to fight the wild man's magic?"

"But you—your parents—"

Had the lord chamberlain suspected all along that Richon might one day inherit his parents' magic? He had never given the least hint of it in all the years that Richon had ruled. He had certainly never encouraged Richon to discover his magic.

Just to see the lord chamberlain's reaction, Richon turned himself into a bear.

It was as he might have expected.

Horror.

The smell of piss.

And then abject groveling. The lord chamberlain actually got onto his knees and wept.

Richon turned himself back into a man. And waited for the lord chamberlain to run out of words.

It took a surprisingly long time.

"You thought to keep me from my magic by keeping me ignorant and afraid, and selfish," said Richon. Though truly he could only blame the lord chamberlain for part of this. The rest of the blame belonged to himself.

"No, no. I did not care about your magic," the lord chamberlain insisted. "I knew that once your parents had been killed you would be easily—" He stopped abruptly, his face gone pale.

"Once my parents were *killed*?" echoed Richon. He had not suspected it at the time, and yet it did not surprise him. Nothing the lord chamberlain had done in his quest for power surprised him now. And the royal steward had been just as ruthless.

"It was the royal steward who hired the men. I could not stop him!" said the lord chamberlain.

Richon played along. "Of course, you tried. You alerted the captain of my father's guard."

"I . . . well . . . I . . . The royal steward would have had me killed." He licked his lips and stared at Richon, as if hoping for mercy.

Richon sighed. He did not know if there was any truth in what the lord chamberlain said. He only knew he did not wish to hear any more of it.

What should be the punishment for such treason? Richon tried to imagine his father in this situation, but of course his father had never inspired men to commit treason.

Still, there had been one man King Seltar had found worthy of a truly terrible punishment. He had been a nobleman who had defiled two young servant girls. The first had not dared to come forward until the second had, and then they came together to corroborate their stories to the king, to ask him for some small sum of money to make recompense for the fact that they would never find a man to marry them because of what the nobleman had done.

The king had listened to them and had given them the sum they asked for times ten. And then he had taken that same amount from the nobleman's wealth and called him to hear why it was done. The nobleman had expected to be given the chance to excuse himself, to beg forgiveness. It was what King Seltar had always done, in Richon's memory.

But instead King Seltar sentenced him to death.

And still the nobleman had not understood. He had blinked and turned toward the dungeons, expecting to be sent there, that he would have time before he had to face his death. But King Seltar had taken a sword and run the nobleman through. Without another word. When the nobleman had tumbled from the sword, the king had let it fall with him. He had turned away and walked back into the palace, leaving the servants to take care of the body.

And Richon had gaped at his kind father and wondered if another soul had possessed him at that moment.

He had never seen anything like the anger on his father's face that day, and he had thought perhaps he had imagined it.

But now he knew he had not, for he felt the same anger himself. There was no remedy for this, no forgiveness possible. This offense was a personal one, and no public trial was necessary.

Richon lifted his sword and ran the lord chamberlain through. It only took strength, not skill, for this.

The traitor gave one bubble of complaint, then lay dead among the others.

Richon left the sword where it was, as his father had,

and walked back to his own men, who celebrated the end of the war, shouting congratulations to each other, slapping backs and falling down in tears and laughter and rejoicing. Those who had been dead spoke of the animals healing their wounds, then remaining for the duration of the battle to make the humans stronger, fiercer, and wilier. But afterward the animal spirits had departed, leaving the humans whole but no longer magically enhanced.

The story made Richon smile and weep at once. There was no promise that the revived men would live out the remainder of their lives. There might yet be a price to be paid for the animals' gift of magic. But for now, to see so many of his men living was enough to make him feel all his guilt washed clean.

Now he had to decide what to do next. He had never allowed himself to think this far ahead, because it seemed impossibly unlikely that he would win this battle and survive with so many of his people. He thought perhaps he could go back to the palace quietly and show his people gradually the kind of man—and king—he could become.

But as he was moving across the battlefield, he was stopped by one of the men who had been dead and touched with the spirit of a wolf (for Richon could still see the faint green outline of the creature on him). The man seemed fierce and Richon held back in fear, but then he called out to the others around him.

"The king! The king has led us to triumph!"

Richon changed into a bear, to disguise himself.

But it had the opposite effect than he had intended. The men around him shouted at him. "It's the king! He's the bear! He came to help us! It's his magic at last!"

Richon turned himself back into a man then, thinking to argue that he only resembled the king.

But by then he was being lifted on shoulders, carried about, and sung to. Terrible songs with lyrics sung by men with voices that were torn and weary.

It was a kind of music he had never heard before. It was made for him, as king, but not because it was due him. Rather because he'd earned it.

Richon was so caught up in the celebration, in the passing of bottles of wine and ale, that he forgot for a moment about the royal steward. When at last he remembered, he asked all around, but no one had seen the man since the battle.

He cursed himself for his lack of focus. He had allowed a few cheers and his own satisfaction at having dispatched one traitor to distract him from chasing the other. He had to find the royal steward and see him pay for his crimes.

He meant to have the hound go with him, and he searched through the battlefield in the dark, calling for her. But she, too, was gone. He did not know where. Had she left him and returned to the forest? Was she hurt? Killed?

He turned into a bear briefly and caught her scent.

As he followed it past the edge of the battlefield, he discovered that it was mingled with the scent of the royal steward.

He turned back into a man and smiled to himself. She had gone after the royal steward!

No doubt she was perfectly capable of taking care of herself, as she had proved more than once, but he felt a twinge of concern, for the royal steward was dangerously clever and had no love for those with animal magic.

In the morning Richon went back to his men and told them they were free to go home, and to take with them any supplies they wished, from livestock to swords, clothing, wood, or wagons.

He was cheered for this, and more than one man came to offer his service to Richon, for whatever was needed. Richon directed this man and others back to the palace. He needed people who were loyal to him there, and he did not much care if they had been wellborn or not. He cared that they were good and that they respected animal magic, as he did now.

He promised to be there soon himself.

With Chala at his side.

Chapter Thirty-nine
The Hound

AFTER FILLING HER stomach, the hound went back to wait outside the inn. It was one of the most difficult things she had ever done. If only she could have simply leaped through the window and attacked. That was what the hound in her longed to do. No thinking about choices, about chances. Do it, or don't do it. But don't stew over it like a human.

Perhaps it would help if she were not so torn between the two sides of herself.

She tried changing herself back to a woman, wondering if that would help her to be more patient. It did not.

So she watched as a hound while the shadows of the royal steward and the cat man sat by the hearth late into the night. And then at last went up to their rooms to sleep.

At dawn her legs were cramped and tight. Her head

was hot and heavy. And her magic was itching to be used.

But she could do nothing as spectacular as what Richon had done. She did not have the magic that he had taken from the animals who had died at the hands of the cat man. She had only her own magic, and little experience with that.

Who was she to stand against the cat man? Why did she not flee back to Richon and tell him of the danger, and warn him to keep himself and those he loved as far from the cat man as he could?

Because she could not do it. Hound or woman, she was too strong and too stubborn to back away from a battle. And perhaps because, like the cat man, she was made of two parts, she was meant to stand against him.

Even if she had no hope of defeating him.

It was nearly midday when she saw the royal steward emerge from the stairs and call for breakfast. A serving girl at the inn brought it to him and he ate near the window. His expression seemed bitter.

It was at least another hour before the cat man appeared. Perhaps because of his unmagic, he appeared exactly as he had when the hound had seen him last, two hundred years hence, down to his chilling smile.

She had seen that smile before, when he had destroyed the spot in her own forest, and when he had followed her to the bear's cave. It was a smile of joyful destruction.

The serving girl was gone when the cat man stopped in the middle of a conversation he was having with the royal steward. He leaned over the royal steward and put a hand on his arm.

And the hound felt the cold of the cat man's unmagic.

The royal steward's face froze. Then crumpled. Then began to turn to dust that fell to the floor in a heap that could have been the ashes from a very small fire.

The supposed ally of the cat man was dead, as simple as that. He had caused so much trouble in Richon's kingdom, but in the end he was nothing.

As if he had never been.

The hound could tell Richon that much at least, if she ever saw him again. He need not fear that the royal steward had escaped, or that he had not suffered enough. An end like this was worse even than a painful death in her mind.

She moved away from the window for a moment to catch her breath, and to save herself from having to look into the face of the cat man any longer. She knew the story, knew how the cat man had been abused by the magic and by a human, but still it seemed to her that his corruption had gone beyond any reasonable revenge.

He had to be stopped, and it was left to her to do it. She had not said a farewell to Richon before she left the battlefield. If she had, he would not have let her go. She had done the right thing, and so had he.

The cat man was standing in the window, staring out at her.

Did he sense her?

He did not smile or try to signal her or speak to her. Just stared.

The hound kept very still.

Could he use his unmagic on her from there? She had felt it, but it seemed he had to touch her to send it out. That was the way it had worked before, when she had seen him in the forest. And with the royal steward.

She could feel no sympathy for the cat man. She wanted only to see his end.

Despite the shaking in her legs, she stood and turned her face away from him to the sky. Then she howled, as a hound would howl. A call to challenge, to battle, to death.

The cat man answered her call by coming out of the inn to meet her.

They stood face-to-face and the cat man smiled again, and reached for her.

She could have stepped away, but she did not. She moved forward and allowed his hand to touch her back.

How it hurt!

The unmagic was terrible enough when it touched the ground she walked across. But this was inside her, not to be turned away from, never to be escaped. It burned and cut through her vitals. She thought she had no more heart to beat, no more lungs to pump air.

She could hear the cat man's soft laughter. "You do not fight against me at all. Do you wish for death, then?"

And the hound found it in herself to spit and stiffen and to feel that she still had a body, though she did not know how. It took her another moment to find her magic and to pull it around herself like a cloak. It was not enough.

As she expected, the cat man's unmagic burned through.

She pulled up her magic once more. This time she did not use it as a defense, but pressed it into the cat man. As she did so, she thought of all the moments that had made her life precious and sharp with joy.

Her first hunt.

Her first coupling with her mate.

The birth of her daughter.

The first sight of the princess.

The smell of the bear in the cave.

The wild man's gap in time.

Her new body.

Her own magic.

And now this.

Even this pain was life. She savored it, and pressed that feeling against the cat man.

This was her magic, and she poured it into him until he drowned in it. It had been so long since he felt true magic, and even then it had not been magic like this.

As she touched him, she saw also his plans for the future. To go south, to conquer animals and humans there, then to return north when he had enough unmagic to finish the destruction completely. It was not only this kingdom that he had threatened. His plan had been an ambitious one, almost like a man's.

The hound drained him of all memories, of all hatred, of all he had been.

Then he was a cat again. The creature in her arms gasped and choked, but there was still some life in it.

The hound was nearly drained herself. She knew it would take all of her magic to finish him. When she was done, she would no longer be able to change between forms. She did not think about it but simply let the magic drain out of her.

And as she did so, she changed once more into a human woman, still in her filthy gown. She was only partly surprised that in her deepest self she was now human.

The cat shivered once as the last of Chala's magic was pressed into him, then sagged against her.

Pulling away from him, damp with human sweat, constricted by the tight bands of fabric around her chest, Chala did not regret her choice.

The wonderful new power she had shared with Richon, to change freely from animal to human, had not lasted long, after all. And now she had given it up, not for him or his kingdom, but for the future world that would have been threatened by the cat man's continued existence.

To no longer be a hound, that was a loss she would have to come to accept. But to never be human again, to lose Richon, to return to what she had been—she could never have come to accept that.

CHAPTER FORTY

Richon

FOLLOWING HER SCENT, Richon came upon Chala the next day. She was carrying water from the well to the inn, looking like a peasant girl with her bucket in hand.

"What happened?" Richon demanded. Something had changed in her, but he was not sure what it was. He feared it had to do with the royal steward she had been chasing and the unmagic he could smell all around him.

Chala told him the fate of the royal steward and of the cat man.

"Then—the unmagic is gone?" he asked, astonished.

"The cat man is gone," said Chala. "But the unmagic will always exist. We have only staved it off. Remember what the wild man said? The battle between magic and unmagic goes on until the end of time."

"But we have done our part for this time," said Richon. The cat man would not be able to spread his unmagic into the future. And for his part, Richon would make sure that the hatred against those with magic was also tempered.

All was well.

Richon breathed deeply, then reached for Chala. He wanted to fold her into his arms and tell her that he loved her. Now he could. He had the words for it, and he meant it truly.

But when he touched her, he felt an emptiness in her that made him draw back. There was more to the story of the cat man's defeat.

"I used my magic against him," said Chala. "All of it. That is how I defeated him. He swallowed it up. I could not battle the unmagic. I could only heal it with as much of my own power as he had of his."

"But you will get it back," said Richon. "Your magic—" He thought of the joy she had in being a hound, chasing through the woods, eating fresh meat, standing at his side when he was a bear.

Was all that lost?

She nodded sadly.

"Never?" he asked.

She shook her head. "My magic is gone. I am a human like those of Prince George's time, who had no magic of their own. Who feel nothing in the woods and have no bond with animals."

Richon began to understand her sacrifice. "I am sorry," he said. He had restored his kingdom, but at what cost to himself? Had he lost her?

"I will go away if you wish it," she said. "I can no longer change into a hound, so I will have to live as a human. But it need not be here if it bothers you. I am strong, at least, and can make my own place in the world." Her chin came up, and Richon could see the Chala he knew. And the hound as well, in her stubborn pride.

"You will go nowhere," he said.

She shifted. "I cannot stay," she said.

"Because of my magic?" Richon asked. If that was so, he would give it all up. He did not know how he could do it. Spread his arms wide and let it go to the forests or the animals? Give it to his people? Or if that did not work, go back to the wild man and beg him to take it? Surely he would have some use for additional magic if he intended to protect the world against unmagic for the rest of time.

"Because I am no longer like you," said Chala. "I have no magic. I cannot change my form. And yet I will always have something of the hound in me."

Richon threw himself forward. He winced at the wrongness of her lack of magic. And then she was in his arms.

She was rigid at first, but gradually seemed to let herself fall into him.

"Is there unmagic?" she asked softly.

"None," Richon assured her.

Chala bowed her head. "There is a scar in me, burned deep. A reminder of what I once had."

Richon was filled with sudden excitement. "I have

enough magic for both of us. I will heal you by giving you of my own." He heard Chala begin to protest, but he ignored her. He reached for both of her arms and held her above the elbows, throwing magic at her.

But it would not enter her. He could feel it bounce off her and return to him, or simply spread out to the world around them—ground, field, forest—where it would be absorbed by whoever happened to walk by it.

He found his fingernails were digging into his hands, and blood was trickling out from his clenched fists.

Chala took his hands in her own and smoothed them out. "I would have told you it was not possible, but I realized you had to see it for yourself."

He sighed. "Then we must both learn to live with it."

"No," she said. "I must learn to live with it. You need do nothing at all."

What did she mean?

Did she think that he would turn away from her now, when he had never felt closer to her? He must make himself more clear.

He reached for her hands and looked into her eyes. "I am not a child who is crying for a sweet fallen in the dirt. I have weathered other changes, and I will weather this one. We will weather it together, you and I. And no doubt it will make us stronger and better, whether we wish to be or not."

There, was that enough for her?

"I can no longer be a hound," she said, very slowly, as if to make sure he could not misunderstand. "If you wish to be a bear and run in the forest, I cannot go with you. You will have to go alone, or find another who can share that part of you."

Richon held her fiercely tight. "I want no other," he said.

"But how can you love a woman who will never again be whole in the way that you are?" she asked. "A woman who will never share your wildness and yet will always wish for it?"

"I love the wound as much as the woman who wears it," said Richon. "And I love the reason she received the wound. How can I ever forget that, when I feel the change in you? You have given so much." He still marveled at it. He had done what he had done to be redeemed, but she had had no mistake to make up for, no honor to be reclaimed.

"And all for me," he added, in awe of her.

"But it was not for you," she said.

He loosened his grip. What did she mean? Had he lost her love somehow? Had she found another here in his kingdom? Who could it be?

"I did what I did because it had to be done," said Chala softly.

Richon was so relieved that he laughed. In a moment, though, the sound turned quickly to choking tears. "And that is why I love you. No selfishness in you at all. It is what I have always aspired to be, and you, Chala, have shown me the way. They should make you king."

"A woman is not a king," said Chala stiffly.

Richon smiled. "Queen, then."

Chala was quiet for a moment. "Are you asking me to marry you?" she said.

Now it was Richon's turn to be quiet. Had it not been obvious to her before? "I do not mean to pressure you," he said at last.

"But I was born a hound," said Chala. "How would your kingdom—"

Richon put a hand over her mouth. Then, when she was silent, he removed it and kissed her. "You are a more human woman than any I have ever found. And I love you."

Tears began to fall down her cheeks.

Richon gathered them one at a time into a cupped palm.

She smiled at last.

"Marry me and make me the happiest man in the world. And my kingdom be hanged if they don't accept you as my queen. They can take us both or send us both on our way. They will survive without us, no doubt. And we will survive without them."

"Truly?" asked Chala. "You would give up your kingdom for me? All these years you wanted nothing more than to be king again, to have another chance."

Richon kissed her again, more desperately. "I have changed," he said.

He convinced Chala eventually, with much kissing. Then there was more kissing and holding, just because there was nothing else he would rather do.

When it was much later in the day, Chala reminded him that he was a king, after all, and didn't he have kingly things to do?

They rested that night in a small forest—hardly more than a few groves of trees next to each other. The following day they saw men from the army returning home all around them. It was difficult for Richon not to stop and greet them all personally. But if he stopped now they would swarm him, and he had no time for that now. So he kept his distance from them, and they were too interested in homecomings to seek him out.

On the third day, Richon and Chala reached the palace. There he spent a few days working in his mother's garden, with Chala's help.

After a week, men began to appear at the palace gates, those Richon remembered from the battlefield and others, asking for work to do. Women came and offered themselves as ladies-in-waiting for Chala. She would not be pampered as Richon would have been tempted to enjoy watching, but she did accept an offer for borrowed gowns. The one she had been wearing since the wild man had changed her was by now completely unsalvageable.

That evening, she took the old gown and put it in a

305

bonfire in the courtyard, along with the broken furniture and reminders of the past that Richon did not wish to keep.

Richon thought she looked as perfect in the new gown as she had in the wild man's, though he noticed both were shades of red. It was, indeed, the most flattering color to her. Had she become human enough to care about something as trivial as that?

"Well, your court will care about it, so I must care about it if I am to be a true queen to you," said Chala when Richon asked her about it.

But he noticed her more than once looking at herself in a passing window, or in a stream. She did not have a mirror in her rooms, however. That much vanity was beyond her.

Richon found that the palace expenses were much decreased from the last time he had been king. The food, prepared by an army cook, was hearty but simple. Hunting parties went out—always without Richon—and brought back meat for those who would eat it. His mother's garden was expanded to include several acres outside the palace.

There were not as many horses, and very little wine drinking or smoking. No balls or celebrations every other day, such as he had lived through before. Richon used the money to pay for reparations to those hurt in the past, and found himself sleeping better at night and feeling more clearheaded every day.

One of the first of those to return to the palace was Jonner, the merchant, who returned a wagonful of books in thanks for the king's saving a cousin's life in the battle. It was such a precious gift that Richon was speechless. He did not know how to express his gratitude. This was a replacement of one of the things that he had missed most.

Then Jonner suggested that Richon allow him to remain in the palace. He had long wished to stop traveling. He was getting older and it did not do his health good to be moving about, never knowing where his next meal or his next bed would come from.

"If you wish to, I suppose we can find a room for you," said Richon.

"A room for me? There is the entire library!" said Jonner, gesturing to it, above the royal suite, a vaste warren of halls and cubbyholes that Richon had let go.

"It is in terrible shape," said Richon. He did not know if the shelves were intact or if any of the other furniture from his parents' library remained in the palace.

"I will rebuild it," said Jonner. "And after that I will sit in it and read all the books I have been meaning to read. Those who wish for knowledge will have only to come to me, and I will direct them to the proper book. I cannot wish for a better life for myself. If it suits you, Your Majesty."

Richon embraced the man heartily. A librarian! Yes, of course. Now his kingdom was complete.

"And I will have a special section for books on magic," said Jonner.

Richon thought of Prince George and his search for any knowledge about the magic. Perhaps that, too, would change in the future.

CHAPTER FORTY-ONE
Chala

THE WEDDING COULD not be escaped. It wasn't the finality of marriage with Richon that bothered Chala. Even the ceremony itself, however tedious and incomprehensible, could be borne. But the preparations made her irritable enough to wish for her hound's teeth, if only to snap at those who bothered her every moment with some triviality.

Already there were rumors swirling that she was a she-bear that Richon had brought back with him from his enchantment. She must do what she could to show her human side as much as possible. And yet there was a part of her that would always be different.

There were three women who became Chala's particular burdens. She refused to call them ladies-in-waiting, for she had no more wish of women fluttering around her now than she had when she had been Princess Beatrice. They were kind enough, but they tended to chatter about topics of no particular interest to Chala. When she spoke of sword fighting, hunting, or running races, they gave her strange looks and seemed to have nothing to add to the conversation.

The three insisted on attending each of Chala's fittings for her wedding gown, for they said that she would not be able to see herself clearly and that they would be better able to tell her what flattered her figure best.

The seamstress came with her best work, but Chala rejected gown after gown. One in particular Chala remembered with a shudder: lace everywhere, with a feathered hat and silver threads that a beautiful white wild bird had died to make.

"You would look like a dainty thing," the seamstress promised as she held it out. "A woman made to adorn the arm of the king."

"It is lovely," said one of the not-ladies-in-waiting.

"Magnificent," said another.

But Chala ignored them. She had not been a human woman long, but she knew what suited her and what did not.

Besides, she did not think that Richon cared a whit about whether or not she looked ornamental on his arm. He had loved her first as a hound, and as a woman he had loved her for what she could do, not for how she looked.

"Bring me something simple," said Chala. She could wear a gown that was striking in color, she had found, but simply designed. Yet she knew that a wedding gown had to be white.

And at last the seamstress returned with a gown that was made of one piece of fabric, from the bodice to the skirt.

"It is from three seasons past," she said, her mouth twisted. "And I never sold it then, for it was too plain for any of the noblewomen who could afford it."

But Chala liked it immediately. It had strong lines and the fabric shimmered when it moved.

She only pulled out the ribbons at the neckline and then raised the gown over her head. She even liked the feel of it as it touched her skin and warmed to her. She smoothed out the fine fabric over her hips.

She looked up and saw the seamstress and the three not-ladies-in-waiting gaping at her.

"It suits her," said the most thoughtful of the three. "With the starkness of the pattern, it is her face you see. The strength in it. And the love."

"She will start a new style entirely," said the seamstress. And she began sketching intently some new gowns that were similar.

So in the end they were not displeased with her choice.

The seamstress brought in a shoemaker later that day. He offered her dainty jeweled slippers and pinched dancing boots with heels too high to be comfortable.

In the end Chala sent him away and decided to wear

instead the boots the wild man's magic had given her when she was first transformed into a woman. They were worn, but she sent them to be cleaned, and they came back shiny and with new laces. They did not show much under the gown, but they did not shame her. And she had the added comfort of knowing that she could run in them.

Not that she expected to need to. But it was nice to know she could all the same.

The morning of the wedding she dressed herself, but allowed one of the ladies to pull her hair back from her face.

Then the music started.

The doors opened.

Chala had to force her legs to move forward.

She had no flowers in her hands. She thought it an abomination to pick living things purely for the sake of decoration.

But now her hands were clenched at her sides.

She was dry-mouthed, staring at Richon, far to the front of the palace chapel. And between the two of them, at least a thousand gaping faces.

She trembled, and tried to decide which way to go.

Toward Richon. Or away from him?

She knew which way she wanted to go. But she did not breathe until she reached his side.

Then he put his hands in hers. "Would it help for you to know that I am dripping sweat?" he said.

It did help. It made her grin and think that perhaps

he sometimes felt as little suited to his role as king as she did to hers as queen.

"Don't look at them. Look at me," he said, pulling her closer. "It's not them you're marrying."

Strangely, as soon as the ceremony was over, the noise of the cheering around her lifted her spirits. She did not mind the cannons firing at all, though dinner went on far too long, and the meat was overcooked.

That night, when at last she went to Richon's bedchamber rather than to her own, he asked her if she was nervous. Many women were, and she was so new to her body, he said.

But she bit his ear and he did not ask any questions after that.

In the morning she woke up with Richon's breath on her shoulder and thought that all had been worth it. Even if she had no moment past this one.

She did mention to him sometime afterward the rumors about her that she had heard whispered about the palace.

Richon went rigid and white with anger. "Who would repeat such things?" he asked. His hands twitched, as if ready for a sword to be placed in them, to defend her honor.

"It is true," said Chala with a shrug. She was surprised that Richon had heard nothing of them himself. It meant something to her that those around him knew him well enough to see how he loved her and how it would hurt him to hear such things.

"It is not true," Richon said flatly. "You are not a bear. You never were one."

"But I was a hound, and I doubt that your people would see much distinction between the two. I was an animal."

"You are human now. As much as any of them," Richon said fiercely. "Without you I do not know if the battle would have gone as it had. I do not know if I would have taken the magic from the animals even. You guided me. And then you ensured that the cat man would never touch us with the unmagic again. You deserve their thanks and their welcome. Not these foul stories."

"I think you must make an announcement of some sort," said Chala.

"And say it is truth? How will that help?"

"It will help because your people will see you as strong enough to stand up against a threat."

"And what of you? If I do as you suggest, then there will be countless jokes told about you all over the kingdom."

"And there are not now?" asked Chala with an arched eyebrow.

"At least they are not said in your hearing," said Richon.

"I think that you can trust me to be formidable enough that that will happen only once," said Chala.

And so it was.

Richon did not make a public announcement, but he spoke openly of Chala's years as a hound at his side and of her transformation.

The week after, a lack-witted noblewoman sat at dinner and mentioned casually that she thought that Chala's teeth were rather large for her face.

Chala opened her mouth very wide and said, "And yet they are perfect for tearing flesh from bones. I always liked the taste of warm blood."

The noblewoman went very still, then left the dinner table after a few minutes and did not return. She left the palace the following day and was not seen again.

Chala was not sorry for her.

But it stopped the rumors.

CHAPTER FORTY-TWO

Richon

IN THE MONTHS following the wedding, peasants came to Richon from far and wide to ask for his wisdom. Others spoke to him of what reasonable taxes might be for the coming year. And many asked if they could send sons, daughters, or cousins to the palace to work.

This was the pleasant side of being king.

There was a far more unpleasant side.

Richon reserved the extreme penalty of execution for those who spread unmagic. There had been death enough in his kingdom already, but he had to send a clear message about not tolerating unmagic if he were to save the future.

Among the first to die was the man from the village with the alehouse who "trained" animals with unmagic. Chala had described him, and then made a positive identification at trial.

Richon told her repeatedly she need not come to the execution, but she insisted upon it.

"I have seen deaths before," she told him.

"But not like this," Richon insisted.

"No? King Helm executed five men while I was his daughter. And he made me come to see each of them. One was a man who did not know he was to be killed. His head was cut off in the midst of a polite conversation about music." She held her lips tightly together when she was done speaking.

Richon thought perhaps she was right. It was not as if she were a sheltered noblewoman. She had seen many things as a hound, and then again when she had been in the body of a princess. And she had been with him at the battle. He did not think this would be worse.

The animal trainer went to his death quietly, and Richon wondered if he was too well acquainted with it by now to fight it. He seemed as empty of life and vigor as any of his animals.

Chala watched it all without any sign of emotion.

But afterward Richon found her weeping in their bedchamber.

"Can I do anything for you?" he asked.

She stared at him, her eyes red. "I understand now," she said.

"Understand what?"

"Guilt," said Chala. "Such a human thing."

Richon nodded soberly.

"It does no good, for it changes nothing. But it is there all the same, reminding you that you might have done something different."

"Not you, Chala," said Richon. "You did all you could."

Chala stared at him. "Are you trying to take away some of my humanness?" she asked.

Richon blanched. "No," he said.

"Then leave me with my guilt."

And he did, but never alone.

What surprised Richon most about being king again was the forest animals that came to consult with him.

A line of them, sometimes as long as the humans who came, would wait and speak to him and wait for him to translate for Chala, for it was her perspective they wished to know. They seemed to see her as their special queen.

Before the wedding and afterward, Richon went out and saw a group of swordsmen practicing in the court-yard. A few of them were soldiers, who used the swords as weapons and thought of death as they wielded them. Others held the swords as if they were artists. All of them were better than he was, so he asked if they would teach him.

He quickly grew stronger. He did not come to like the sword any better than before, however, and wondered if there were another battle, if he would do the same as before and simply turn into a bear.

Chala, however, had no such choice. She practiced

sword fighting with him in the courtyard of the palace and Richon loved to watch her. It was as if she had gained back some of what she had lost in losing her magic: the ferociousness and focus that she had as a hound and the sheer grace of her movements.

Often there was quite a crowd to see Chala best Richon, as she did all too frequently. And Richon heard there were more than a few women who were asking to join his royal guard—or even the army. That was when he felt that his people had truly come to see Chala as he did, as one of them, but more.

It was on one of those sword-fighting mornings when a man galloped forward on a horse, dressed finely in livery, and announced himself as a servant to Lord Kaylar, who had once been one of Richon's companions in drinking and hunting.

Richon had refused many other "friends" from the past who had written to ask for a return to the king's favor. But when Richon opened Lord Kaylar's letter, it was a challenge to a battle to the death, to prove who should be rightful king of Elolira.

"What shall I say to my lord, Kaylar?" asked the messenger.

Richon could not see how he could refuse a challenge from one of his own noblemen. "I accept," he said.

"It is for you to choose the place and time," said the messenger.

Richon nodded. "One week hence. In this courtyard.

At noon." The men around him cheered.

The messenger held himself very still.

"And the weapons?" asked Richon. That was Lord Kaylar's choice.

"Magic," said the messenger.

"Very well, then, magic it is," said Richon. He had never seen a battle of magic before, though he had read of them in books that Jonner had recently shown him. It was an ancient tradition.

The messenger promptly mounted his horse and went galloping back in the direction from which he had come.

"Lord Kaylar?" asked Chala later, when the two of them were alone together.

"Yes," said Richon. "Why?" She couldn't know of the man, could she?

"He is the one," said Chala.

"Which one?"

She only had to say one word. "Crown."

Richon hissed, as the invitation suddenly made sense to him. Lord Kaylar had been the sort of man who attacked where he knew he would win. If he had been angry at Richon, he would attack him through his horse.

Poor Crown.

What did Lord Kaylar intend to do now? Richon suspected the man must have magic himself, but perhaps not much. In order to maim a horse as he did Crown, he could not feel much of the animal's pain.

So why would he choose to battle with magic?

Did he think to prove that Richon did not have much of it, either? Or prove that Richon was a coward if he refused to kill a man with it?

Doubts tumbling in his mind, Richon did not sleep well for the next week. But when the day came, he was waiting in the courtyard as Lord Kaylar arrived, complete with his entourage. There was a banner-carrying young page at the front, in the bright colors of blue and gold that were Lord Kaylar's. Then came the men-at-arms, who rode on warhorses. There were six of them.

Then Lord Kaylar himself, astride the largest horse of all. And after that, two carriages full of his wife and her ladies-in-waiting, who had come to watch the "sport" of seeing Lord Kaylar attempt to kill the king with his magic.

"My lord," said Richon with a nod.

Lord Kaylar stared ahead coldly.

Then Richon put out his hands so that his own people would step back and give them space. When they were far enough away, he began to change into a bear.

He looked at Lord Kaylar. It seemed his magic was taking him much longer to use. Well, the bear would wait for it, then. He would not wish to be called unfair.

He stepped back.

And saw the man reach for a sword thrown toward him by one of his men.

The bear had no chance to see how an animal without a weapon would fare in a battle against a man with one.

Chala raced between Lord Kaylar and Richon and struck Lord Kaylar through the heart with her own sword.

When he lay dead at Richon's feet, she turned up to look at him.

"I think King Helm would be proud of his princess," Richon said.

Chala stared at her bloodstained hands. "I think not. It is not what a princess would do."

"Perhaps not. But shouldn't a queen do all she can to defend her king—and her people?" Richon asked.

"I would never have done it as a hound," Chala said. "I would have thought my strength would show your weakness."

"Your strength is my strength," said Richon. "And it always will be."

"Thank you," said Chala.

Lord Kaylar's entourage left swiftly.

Afterward, the others in the courtyard lifted Chala to their shoulders and sang warrior songs to her.

They howled to the skies and Chala did not join in. She seemed very thoughtful.

That night she said to Richon, "I thought I had lost my pack. But I have found it again."

Epilogue

KING RICHON AND Queen Chala ruled happily for many years, though they were not blessed with a child to rule after them. Some said it was because the king's magic was too strong for any child to hold. Others said that it was part of the curse that had made the king into a bear.

But it was the queen who seemed most hurt by her childlessness. She was often seen among the children of the palace, playing games with them, throwing a ball in the air and catching it with her teeth, or teaching them the foolish rules of being human that their parents expected them to learn without speaking of them.

When the king grew older, he went on a journey to the far reaches of the kingdom and brought back with him a young woman named Halee, who had as much of the magic as the king himself did, though it seemed to have come to her late in life. She had compassion as well, which the king thought far more important to being a good ruler. In time the king named her his heir.

The king and queen stayed for several months to help her learn all she needed, and then they disappeared one night and were never seen again in that land or that time. It is said that they returned to their animal forms and that they are still to be seen on the darkest of nights in the forest, where the magic is strong.

But the truth is that they returned to the wild man in the mountains.

He was waiting for them, lying on a blanket, his head tilted to one side and his eyes closed.

At first Chala thought he was dead. The smell of death was in the air. It was part of the reason that she and Richon had come to him now. Richon had noticed it as far away as the palace, and even Chala had begun to get a sense of it, despite her utter lack of magic after all these years.

But the wild man was still breathing. She could see the rise and fall of his chest.

"Ah," he said, opening his eyes and struggling to sit up.

Richon moved to help him.

How frail the wild man had grown, thought Chala. He looked more wolf than man now, with those huge teeth and the skin sunken around his eyes making them look brighter than ever before.

"You have come," he whispered.

"We could not have done otherwise," said Richon. "Not when I heard your call."

"Your kingdom?" asked the wild man.

"In the care of one who loves the magic as only one who thought she did not have it can," said Richon.

The wild man nodded. "Good."

"I cannot thank you enough," said Richon.

The wild man smiled widely, like a wolf. "You will not say that when you hear what it is I have brought you here to do," he said.

Richon waited.

But Chala thought she already knew.

"The magic needs protecting, and I can no longer do it, but you can," said the wild man to Richon.

"But I—I could not possibly take your place. You have so much magic—" Richon sputtered.

"You have as much magic as I did when I began," said the wild man. "But that is not why I ask you to take my place. There are others who are strong enough, but they do not understand how important it is, how horrible the unmagic will be. You do."

Richon stopped protesting. "I do," he said.

"And she will stay with you," said the wild man, gesturing to Chala.

"Without magic?" asked Richon. He was as pale as he had been when he first realized what Chala had given up to destroy the cat man.

Chala put a hand to the back of his neck to reassure him. She did not mind.

"Here, alone, for years on end?" said Richon.

"Ah, but she will not be without magic," said the wild man.

Richon stared.

And Chala, for the first time, felt hope in her heart.

"I will give her my magic," said the wild man. "Mine alone is old enough to work past the scar of the unmagic in her. And to enable her to have a child again, when the time comes."

"A child?" said Richon, eyes wide.

It was then that Chala saw the pain he had concealed for so long, so as to avoid adding to hers. How much he had wanted the child that she could not give him. The scar in her had not only walled off her magic, but had made her unable to engender any life, for magic is life.

"Come to me," said the wild man.

Chala approached him. She had never felt so light, and so afraid. She had had a child before and Richon had not. She knew the love a child would bring into their lives as well as the pain.

The wild man put his hands on her.

She felt the rush of magic into her, sweet and hot, like love itself.

Then the magic was hers and the wild man was falling away from her.

Richon's smile—when she touched him and he felt her magic—was all the reward she could have asked for.

Together they found rocks under which to bury the wild man's body. He would be remembered, in legends and in their own minds.

But life went on, and so did magic.

METTE IVIE HARRISON has a PhD in Germanic literature and is the author of THE PRINCESS AND THE HOUND; MIRA, MIRROR; and THE MONSTER IN ME.

Of THE PRINCESS AND THE BEAR, she says, "I never thought there would be a sequel to THE PRINCESS AND THE HOUND, but when I read through the galleys, I realized that there was another book waiting in the story of the bear and the hound. In some ways, you might think of it more as a parallel novel than as a sequel, because it stands on its own as a new story. But who knows? Maybe I'll look at these galleys and find another story demanding to be told."

She lives with her family in Utah.

You can visit her online at www.metteivieharrison.com.

The Princess and the Bear

A Q&A with Mette Ivie Harrison

An Imagining of George and Marit's Future

A sneak peek at *The Princess and the Snowbird*

A Q&A with Mette Ivie Harrison

What was the hardest part about writing *The Princess and the Bear*?

I wrote the first draft in a rush in one month, but it was nearly a year before I was ready to send it to an editor, because it needed A LOT of editing. I knew I wanted it to be about the hound and the bear from *The Princess and the Hound*, but I really only had Richon's story in my head at first. When I looked back at the revision with some objectivity a few months after that first draft, I could see clearly that Chala didn't have a story of her own. She was following Richon around as his companion, and she had alternating chapters with her POV, but she didn't have her own quest. Really that is what makes a character interesting: how they struggle against their limitations and ultimately become victorious. So I had to figure out how Chala's adventure could happen at the same time as Richon's and then make both stories into a single book. It was tricky.

What makes a good romance?

I spent a lot of time trying to figure out what the formula of a great romance is. Witty, unforgettable dialog like Jane Austen? Terrible dilemmas like Megan Whalen Turner? Problems like Lois McMaster Bujold? Utter devotion like Jim Butcher's Harry Dresden? What I finally figured out was that there is no formula for true romance. The trick to making a reader believe that two characters will fall in love with each other is to make the reader fall in love with both characters. How do you do that? You make the characters deeply

3

good and then throw them into an impossible situation. They will find each other. I think people like that really do, in real life. The best romance is one that is utterly unique and that would fit no one else. After all, who could love and live with someone like Chala? Only Richon. But that doesn't mean it would be easy.

What makes a good fantasy?
I tend to prefer fantasy with strong characters and less reliance on the fantastic. For me, fantasy is about exploring what people would be like if the reality of life were a little bit different. It's a "What If?" question. I also try hard to make my fantasy readable, so that there are not a lot of new words in italics in the first few pages. That seems to make it more difficult for readers to get into a fantasy because they have to invest so much mental energy to understand what is going on. Also, when there are perfectly good English words for a given thing, it makes no sense to make up another one just for the sake of writing in a magical language. Thus "animal magic" is exactly what it sounds like it is. I could have made up a word for it like "ewoll," but then I'd have to spend time explaining what "ewoll" is, which would be "ewoll is the ability to communicate with animals magically." I couldn't see the value in that.

I will also say that I think one thing that distinguishes fantasy from realistic fiction is that the climax in fantasy is really, really big. I hope that it feels like a very human climax, that it isn't just a battle scene with lots of blood and gore, but that it's also a climax about finding yourself and the pain of giving up what you used to be. But if you don't have a battle or some magical revelation, I'm not sure

4

you have a fantasy. At least, not my kind of fantasy. I think that *The Princess and the Bear* is at the same time a double coming-of-age story, a romance, and an epic fantasy. It's about finding out who you are, making recompense, finding love, and saving the world.

What are some of your favorite books?
Here is a short list:

Shannon Hale's *Book of a Thousand Days*
Megan Whalen Turner's *The Queen of Attolia*
Ysabeau S. Wilce's *Flora Segunda*
Edith Pattou's *East*
Sherwood Smith's *Crown Duel*
Elizabeth Marie Pope's *The Perilous Gard*
Tamora Pierce's *Lady Knight*
Gail Carson Levine's *Ella Enchanted*
Martine Leavitt's *Keturah and Lord Death*

For more recommendations, go to
www.metteivieharrison.com.

What happens to George and Marit in the new future?
I like to imagine that George and Marit meet in very much the same circumstances in the future that would happen after *The Princess and the Bear*. The details change because the animal magic isn't as prohibited, but that doesn't mean life will be easy for them.

An Imagining of George and Marit's Future

Richon could hear the animals call to him from across the distance of two kingdoms. There was a terrible battle being fought, and magic was on both sides.

It should not be so. There was unmagic enough to destroy magic. No need for magic to work against itself.

But it was.

Prince George was at the head of one army; the boy the bear had known as Soren at the other.

Richon transformed himself into a bear and ran with the hound, never stopping for more than enough time to drink from a stream and to fall into it in exhaustion, until the cool water woke him again, and pushed him onward.

When they came to the forest by Prince George's castle, the bear ran through it without thinking. It was not until he came to the cave that he realized the change. He stopped, only for a moment, to take in the scent of new plants pushing up through the rich, ash-colored earth around the old stream bed. Perhaps the stream would return, too, someday. And the animals who had once lived here.

The forest had a chance now, to become alive again, where before it had been lost forever.

A bark from the hound brought him back to attention. He did not have time to spend here, not now. The battle was being fought just past the castle, in the open field where Prince George's troops had so often trained for the wars they hoped they would never fight against King Helm of Sarrey.

And they never had. Prince George had warded off that threat well, with his marriage to Princess Marit. But now another threat had risen in its stead.

The bear stood on his hind legs and gathered his last strength. There were no animals here for him to take from, so he was left to his own power. The hound at his side was dripping wet and had lamed her left hind leg. She dragged behind him, insisting that she did not need him to stop, that it was too urgent to go on, that they must do what the wild man would have done in this case—save Prince George from this attack by those who should have supported him.

Outside the forest, Richon could see Prince George's castle. Or what was left of it. The high tower that had always risen above the rest, to signal the castle's presence even in the mistiest of mornings, was gone. Richon blinked and then saw what remained of it, slumped to one side. It looked as though it had been felled by some great flash of lightning. Richon remembered the magicians who claimed to be able to control the weather in his youth. Perhaps it was so in Prince George's time now, as well.

The rest of the castle looked mostly deserted. The drawbridge was up, as Richon had not seen it in all the years he had lived as a bear in the forest here. There were few sounds from inside, but now and again, he saw a small face peeking through a window. Children and no one else, protected by the moat and the bridge, so long as they lasted. Not only children from the castle, Richon guessed, but from the village near it.

At least, that was what Richon would have done, if he were

Prince George and his subjects were in danger. A castle was only a thing. His people were the life of his kingdom. They must be saved first and foremost, and if it cost the castle, so be it.

Richon thought how he had changed, for once in his youth as king he had refused to allow the village children to even come near the palace for the new year's celebration. He had not wanted to be near such poverty, and had worried that the children would remind him of all he had not done for them after his father's death. So the villagers' celebration had been canceled and Richon had instead celebrated with his courtiers, inside his palace, where it was safe.

There.

He could see the armies now, as well as feel them.

They were at battle already.

Prince George was to the left, on a large black horse that seemed restless beneath him. To the right was another man in the same green and black colors of Kendel, but this man was hunched over in his saddle and crowded with other soldiers. It was King Davit, who had hardly left the castle for several years now, due to his illness. He must have insisted on coming to this, though as far as Richon could tell he was doing little for the battle but drawing more fire to himself and those surrounding him than any ordinary man his age and health should have done.

For a man who wished to save himself, it was idiocy. For a man who wished to save his son, and perhaps his kingdom—it was a brilliant self-sacrifice.

The cannons were fired.

The two soldiers to the king's left fell as the cannonball blasted to the ground next to them.

Prince George turned in time to see the smoke. "Father!" he called out, and kneed his horse to get closer. But it was impossible. There were too many others between the king and the prince.

And then the smoke cleared, and King Davit appeared once more. His face was blackened, but he held up his arm in a fist and shook it at the enemy.

The whole army around him was heartened, and cheered.

The bear and the hound moved around from behind. The bear wanted to get close to Prince George, to ask him what he knew.

The two armies seemed well matched. Too well-matched.

The bear noticed that there were animals fighting on only the other side, and they were in front, where they would be killed first. Prince George had not called an animal army to fight for him. There were a few hounds dead at the front of the battle, a male and a female, but no others that Richon could see.

And then he looked closer at them.

He knew those hounds.

They were of the shape-shifting family he and the hound had met as they journeyed to see the wild man so long ago. The mother and father, Frant and Sharla, had been looking for a place to raise their children safely with the magic. A place for them to find others with the magic like themselves, so that their children could marry like to like.

Now they were dead.

And their children?

The bear could only hope that they were back in the castle,

9

safe, and not here in the battle somewhere, fighting on one side—
or the other.

The hound barked once to call the bear's attention to her, and
then the bear saw the princess. She was at Prince George's side,
wearing a helmet and the simple clothing of any other soldier. It
had the advantage of not making her a target to the other army,
Richon supposed. But it also made it impossible for those around
her to protect her specially.

The hound barked once, then seemed to gather strength somehow. She looked at the bear once, and he nodded. No words were
needed. He knew what she must do, just as he knew what he must
do.

The hound broke away from him then, and ducked into spaces
that he as a bear never could. She leaped away from swords, spears
and arrows, until she reached the princess's side. The princess held
a broad sword in her hand, too large for her, the bear thought. But
she seemed comfortable with it.

She nearly cut off the hound's head at her unexpected approach.
Then the princess recognized her hound, her eyes widened and
mouth drew up in an "o." She did not take time to hug her, but there
was a tightening of her lips that seemed to express satisfaction and
after that the princess left her left side open, for the hound to be her
protection there. Then she fought through to the front of the army,
striking animals and men alike dead at her feet.

The bear did not try to make it to the prince's side. He thought
the army would be better served if he fought at the front, directly
against the boy with the red hair who held tight to the mane of a

horse far too large for him. A boy who should not have been in the battle, let alone leading it. And yet, he was winning, for now. Because he was willing to use his magic to force animals to do his will, and kill them.

Prince George was not.

But it was Prince George's army that was retreating, slowly, step by step, but without a doubt as the bear charged at the animals on the front line. The hours went on, and the bear did not even notice anymore what kind of creature it was that he was killing. He leaped, and tore, lunged and cut, threw an arm out and pushed to the ground.

The actions were automatic. He drew on the magic to give himself further strength, taking from the very animals that he meant to kill. They were used to Soren taking their strength from them, but not another. Some did not even live long enough to be killed by the bear with a strike to the head or belly, but simply expired before his eyes, fell, and were trodden over as the army behind them pressed forward.

It was horrible.

The bear had thought the battle between his army and the army of the king of Nolira had been bad enough, but this was between men who should have been brothers, who should have lived together in love and tolerance.

After all he had done to save magic, to save the past so that it could become a brighter future; it seemed he had not done enough. This battle had still come.

A sneak peek at

The Princess and the Snowbird

L IVA DID NOT think of her age in years, for that was a human habit. She did not even think of her age in seasons, because she did not bother to count them—only humans counted. Liva equally enjoyed the bright sky of summer; the wet, verdant green of spring; the colors of autumn; and the darker sky of winter. She did not long for one while she had the other. Each season was its own. There were animals who lived through only one season, and those who lived through many, as she did.

One day Liva sat in her cave, practicing birdcalls as she changed from one form to the next: plover, eider, crake, dovekie, grebe, and dipper. She enjoyed the sensation of one form sliding into the next, and each time she went through the repetition, she sped it up. She was caught in the midst of a transformation when she heard the sound of ragged breathing at the mouth of the cave.

Her mother limped toward her, trailing blood, her hind leg torn so that it hung the wrong way.

"Mother!" Liva called out, taking her mother's shape, the shape of a wild hound, rare in the north. She lunged forward and licked at her mother's wound, but it was too deep to staunch with only her saliva.

"What happened?" Liva asked in the language of the hounds, for it was the only language her mother could now speak, since she had given the great gift of her aur-magic to Liva at birth.

"A white wolf," gasped the hound. "Starving. I should have avoided him. But I have my pride."

"I will kill him," Liva threatened. She leaned forward and sniffed her mother's flank, to get a sense of the white wolf. She was excellent at tracking, and she was certain she would find the wolf not long after she left the cave. If he was hungry, he would make mistakes, and though she was not full grown, she could defeat him.

"No, Liva," said her mother. And then she bit out a cry of pain.

Liva stared at her, frightened. She had never seen her mother unable to control herself this way. "I will!" Liva said. "You cannot stop me. I will do what I want."

"Please," her mother whispered, her head low to the ground, though she did not allow herself to fall to her side. "Stay with me, Liva. I need you with me now."

Liva sighed and put her head under her mother's. "I will go for Father, then," she said. "He will kill the wolf instead, and then he will come and make you well again."

She said this though her father had also given up his aur-magic to his daughter. He had only enough magic to remain a bear, though he had been born a man. In the forest a bear and a hound could protect a child better than humans could, for a hound was fast and had an acute sense of smell, while a bear was very large and had a roar loud enough to shake the river from its banks.

"No," her mother said again. "He is too far away for you to go to him. And he has more important things to do. There are lives that depend on him."

"Your life depends on him," whimpered Liva. She did not like to show her fear. An animal that showed its fear was weak. That was the law of the forest that Liva had learned since she had first begun to take animal shapes as a small child.

"Those with aur-magic in the south are hunted down and if captured put to death. Your father must help them

14

stay free. But I will recover," said her mother. "All I need is time. And you." She nuzzled Liva.

It distracted Liva for a little while. Then her mother quieted and closed her eyes. Her breathing was still sharp and uneven, but Liva thought the hound was asleep.

Liva examined the wound with her eyes, with her nose, and then with her magic. The leg was damaged beyond repair. There were veins that had been cut off, scar tissue forming around muscles that would stiffen them.

Ever since Liva could remember, her mother had refused to take Liva's magic to shape herself into an animal for play. Liva did not understand why. She had plenty of aur-magic for them both, so the only theory that made sense to Liva was that her mother preferred the shape of a hound.

Now Liva put a paw to her mother's leg. The hound winced and tensed up the leg. In that moment, Liva pressed magic into the wound.

But the magic rebounded to her painfully, thrust back by her mother. "Liva, leave it be," said the hound, opening her eyes for just a moment, as if she were too tired to do so for long.

Liva was confused. "I can fix your wound," she said. "I can. I can see how to do it." Could she be afraid that Liva would damage her leg?

"I do not doubt it," said her mother. "But you must not use your magic on me."

15

"It is not just for play," Liva insisted.

"No, but I've had my chance with the aur-magic already." The hound's words were slurred, and it seemed to Liva as though she was only partly herself. Surely that must be why she was not making any sense.

"Just a little," said Liva, persisting. Her father had tried that on her, when she was ill, and he wanted her to take in some broth. She had taken a single sip, just to stop the noise of his pleading. But then she had found that it tasted wonderful, that the warmth that struck her stomach was just what she could have wished for, so she had taken more and more.

"None," said her mother, growling at her.

So Liva left the cave. She hunted for dinner, and brought back some of the carcass for her mother. Her mother would not touch the meat. She was too weak, and turned to her other side, sleeping heavily. The hound would not stir even when Liva tried to wake her to move closer to the far side of the cave.

Instead Liva pulled the furs over from the far side of the cave. She draped them around her mother's shoulders, changing into human form briefly because human hands were the most useful for this task.

Then she changed back into a hound and cuddled close to her mother, her back to her mother's front. She fell asleep for a time that way, until she was woken in the middle of the night by the sound of her mother's weeping.